Samuel French Acting Edition

Bernhardt/Hamlet

by Theresa Rebeck

SAMUELFRENCH.COM   SAMUELFRENCH.CO.UK

FOR PRODUCTION ENQUIRIES

UNITED STATES AND CANADA
Info@SamuelFrench.com
1-866-598-8449

UNITED KINGDOM AND EUROPE
Plays@SamuelFrench.co.uk
020-7255-4302

Each title is subject to availability from Samuel French, depending
upon country of performance. Please be aware that *BERNHARDT/
HAMLET* may not be licensed by Samuel French in your territory.
Professional and amateur producers should contact the nearest Samuel
French office or licensing partner to verify availability.

MUSIC USE NOTE

Licensees are solely responsible for obtaining formal written permission from copyright owners to use copyrighted music in the performance of this play and are strongly cautioned to do so. If no such permission is obtained by the licensee, then the licensee must use only original music that the licensee owns and controls. Licensees are solely responsible and liable for all music clearances and shall indemnify the copyright owners of the play(s) and their licensing agent, Samuel French, against any costs, expenses, losses and liabilities arising from the use of music by licensees. Please contact the appropriate music licensing authority in your territory for the rights to any incidental music.

IMPORTANT BILLING AND CREDIT REQUIREMENTS

If you have obtained performance rights to this title, please refer to your licensing agreement for important billing and credit requirements.

BERNHARDT/HAMLET was commissioned and originally produced by Roundabout Theatre Company (Todd Haimes, Artistic Director; Harold Wolpert, Managing Director; Julia C. Levy, Executive Director; Sydney Beers, General Manager) in New York, NY, premiering on September 25, 2018 at the American Airlines Theatre. The performance was directed by Moritz von Stuelpnagel, with sets by Beowulf Boritt, costumes by Toni-Leslie James, and lighting by Bradley King. The production stage manager was James FitzSimmons. The cast was as follows:

SARAH BERNHARDT	Janet McTeer
CONSTANT COQUELIN	Dylan Baker
EDMOND ROSTAND	Jason Butler Harner
ALPHONSE MUCHA	Matthew Saldivar
MAURICE	Nick Westrate
LOUIS / ENSEMBLE	Tony Carlin
ROSAMOND	Ito Aghayere
LYSETTE	Brittany Bradford
RAOUL	Aaron Costa Ganis
FRANÇOIS / WORKER	Triney Sandoval
ENSEMBLE	Matthew Amendt, Jenelle Chu, Kate Levy, Chris Thorn

CHARACTERS

SARAH BERNHARDT
CONSTANT COQUELIN
EDMOND ROSTAND
ALPHONSE MUCHA
MAURICE
LOUIS
ROSAMOND
LYSETTE
RAOUL
FRANÇOIS
WORKER

SETTING

1897, Paris

ACT ONE

Scene One

(The stage.)

*(**SARAH**, as Hamlet, light on her in darkness. As the lights rise we see a company of actors watching her, rapt.)*

SARAH. O what a rogue and peasant slave am I!
　　Is it not monstrous that this player here,
　　But in a fiction, in a dream of passion,
　　Could force his soul...

(She stops, thinking.)

CONSTANT. *(Sotto voce, prompting.)* ...So to his own conceit –

SARAH. So to his own conceit!

CONSTANT. That from her working –

SARAH. That from her – working –

CONSTANT. All his visage waned –

SARAH. Visage waned? Is that it? Seriously?

CONSTANT. That's it.

SARAH. Are you sure?

CONSTANT. I've done it –

SARAH. Who's got the pages?

CONSTANT. Four times.

*(**LYSETTE** brings **SARAH** the pages.)*

SARAH. Yes we know.

CONSTANT. Tears in his eyes –

SARAH. I know, Constant –
　　*(To **LYSETTE**.)* No, this is Act One –

LYSETTE. Is it?

> *(They are looking for the spot in the script.)*

CONSTANT. *(Showing off now.)* Distraction in his aspect,
A broken voice and his whole function suiting
With forms to his conceit?

SARAH. Yes I have it Constant I have the words it's the sense of it that eludes. I cannot make it out! "Is it not monstrous that this player here but in a fiction, in a dream of passion could force his soul so to his own conceit," how is that monstrous. He is a player. It is what players do.

CONSTANT. Yes of course but he himself cannot do it.

SARAH. Because he is not a player.

CONSTANT. "Yet I,
A dull and muddy-mettled rascal, peak
Like John-a-drams, unpregnant of my cause" –

SARAH. "Unpregnant"? Now you're just making up words.

CONSTANT. "And can say nothing." Yes, that's his point. The players can act, why can't he?

SARAH. It is a lot of words for such a small thought.

LYSETTE. You spoke it beautifully, Madame Sarah.

SARAH. He speaks and speaks but does nothing. It is so ponderous. Oh well. We're going to have to back up.

FRANÇOIS. Where from?

SARAH. Well, the entrance.

FRANÇOIS. That far?

SARAH. It went off somewhere.

LYSETTE. Was I over here?

SARAH. Let's try all three of you downstage.

FRANÇOIS. It's not what we did.

SARAH. Well, let's do it now, and see how it works.

FRANÇOIS. All right, but it's not what we did.

SARAH. That's why we're going to try it and see how it works. Constant you too you too.

CONSTANT. You can't put everyone in the same corner.

SARAH. Oh my god. Must everyone argue with every word out of my mouth today?

RAOUL. Are we all going to enter from the same place? What if I came from up. Like way up.

(He points toward the stairs.)

SARAH. Good. François, go with him.

CONSTANT. If it's one company wouldn't they all arrive together?

FRANÇOIS. They're late.

RAOUL. They stopped for a cup of wine.

FRANÇOIS. *(Agreeing with this.)* They stopped for a cup of wine!

SARAH. I like it. They're a little drunk.

CONSTANT. A little drunk? Why not just give them license to steal. They're upstaging you already.

(For the two guys are laughing, drunken.)

SARAH. No one upstages me.

(This is severe. Then she laughs. They all laugh.)

CONSTANT. This would be my point.

SARAH. We have to do something to perk this scene up if Hamlet is just going to drone.

EDMOND. *(Entering.)* Hamlet?

SARAH. Edmond!

(The others greet him with deference.)

CONSTANT. Monsieur.

LYSETTE. Monsieur Rostand.

SARAH. You're back from the country, finally!

EDMOND. *(Looking around.)* What are you doing?

CONSTANT. Hamlet.

FRANÇOIS. Hamlet.

RAOUL. Hamlet.

EDMOND. You're doing Hamlet?

SARAH. The Prince of Denmark. Do you like it?

> *(She models her costume for him.)*

EDMOND. Very fetching. Hamlet!

> *(She gives him the script.)*

SARAH. Here, we made it all the way up to "O what a rogue and peasant slave" and it completely fell apart.

CONSTANT. She doesn't have the lines.

SARAH. I do have the lines.

LYSETTE. *(To* **EDMOND.***)* She doesn't have them.

SARAH. I have them! They confound me but I have them. Here it is.

> *(She shows him the speech.)*

O, what a rogue and peasant slave am I!
Is it not monstrous that this player here,
But in a fiction, in a dream of passion,
Could force his soul so to his own conceit
That from her working all his visage wann'd,
Tears in his eyes, distraction in's aspect,
A broken voice, and his whole function suiting
With forms to his conceit? And all for nothing!
For Hecuba!
What's Hecuba to him, or he to Hecuba,
That he should weep for her? What would he do
Had he the motive and the cue for passion
That I have? He would drown the stage with tears
And cleave – Oh, damn –

CONSTANT. *(Prompting.)* Cleave the general ear.

SARAH. Cleave the general ear!

CONSTANT. With horrid speech.

SARAH. With horrid speech.

CONSTANT. Make mad the guilty.

SARAH. Make mad the guilty.

CONSTANT. And appall the free –

SARAH. And appall the – I can't – what is he saying?

EDMOND. How can you not know? You've done it three times.

SARAH. Only as Ophelia and she isn't in this bit. "Cleave the general ear with horrid speech." Horrid speech, what's so horrid about it? And if he doesn't like it, why does he write so very much of it? You're a playwright, explain.

EDMOND. That's not what he's saying.

CONSTANT. It is actually. He respects the players but not the play.

EDMOND. That is the opinion of a mere player.

SARAH. We are all mere players.

(General approval from all.)

FRANÇOIS. Are we working?

SARAH. Yes we are. Someone bring Monsieur Rostand a chair.

(One of the others brings a chair.)

EDMOND. *(Impressed and surprised.)* You're actually doing Hamlet.

SARAH. Is there something mystifying about the costume?

EDMOND. No. No.

SARAH. Am I a coward?

(Trying it several ways.) Am I a coward. Am I a coward?

(Then.)

(To **EDMOND.***)* Am I a coward? Who calls me villain?

(She looks at **EDMOND,** *asking these questions directly.)*

Breaks my pate across, plucks off my beard and blows it in my face? You see, this is what I mean about this speech which by the way I do have.

(Hands the script back to **EDMOND.***)*

Why need we a beard? Hamlet has no beard.

EDMOND. Shakespeare has given him a beard.

SARAH. He has not given him anything. We give him, the players give him life. He is words on a page, without the life.

(*The players cheer this.*)

EDMOND. That is arrogant in the extreme.

SARAH. No, the question is a good one.

EDMOND. The question is inane, Sarah!

SARAH. Now I am "inane." The greatest actress of the century. The greatest, most arrogant actress in Paris. Europe some would say, to the resounding grief of the impeccable Duse.

(*She is playing to the other actors, who have settled in to watch the debate.*)

But Monsieur Rostand in his wisdom deems me "ridiculous" and "inane."

CONSTANT. We taking a break?

EDMOND. Yes you are taking a break.

SARAH. We are rehearsing!

EDMOND. While you rehearse they can smoke a cigarette.

SARAH. You are not in command of my rehearsal!

EDMOND. All you're doing is talking about whether or not Hamlet has a beard. I think they can take a break.

SARAH. I order you to leave.

(**EDMOND** *starts to go.*)

(*Impatient.*) Not you! Them!

(*They go.*)

EDMOND. You're such a tyrant.

SARAH. There are many fascinating tyrants in Shakespeare. I missed you. What have you been doing?

EDMOND. I'm writing a new play.

SARAH. I want to see it!

EDMOND. It's not ready. But this!

(He looks around.)

SARAH. My new theater is beautiful, is it not?

EDMOND. Big.

SARAH. Yes. That should get their attention.

EDMOND. Hamlet will get their attention.

SARAH. It will; yes, it will.

EDMOND. Might I point out, you cannot attempt to play Hamlet as an act of ego, Sarah.

SARAH. All of theater is an act of ego. If I am celebrated the world over as the greatest actress alive, that is not because my ego has failed me.

(She starts to play it to him.)

O, what a rogue and peasant slave am I! Is it not monstrous that this player here, but in a fiction, a dream of passion...

(Then.)

You know though, I really do have a question about that beard.

EDMOND. It's a metaphor.

SARAH. Not a very good one. I'm taking it out. He is a nineteen-year-old boy, he wouldn't even have a beard.

EDMOND. He is thirty.

SARAH. We are told endlessly how young he is!

EDMOND. "Alas poor Yorick. I knew him, Horatio."

SARAH. I do know the lines, and I tell you, he is away at university when his father is murdered. He is seventeen.

EDMOND. Yorick has been in the ground twenty-three years!

SARAH. Another example of how careless Shakespeare is.

(She goes to him, runs her hand on his face.)

I don't care what Shakespeare thinks. I don't like beards.

(Looks at him.)

I don't like your hair either.

EDMOND. You don't like my hair!

SARAH. What have you done to it. No no. You's a brilliant writer. A writer's hair should be more...disheveled.

(She messes up his hair.)

EDMOND. I am not a character in your play, Sarah.

SARAH. If you were, your hair would look better. And you would not stay in the country so long.

EDMOND. Well, if you were a character in my play –

SARAH. I am often characters in your plays.

EDMOND. Stop interrupting. If you were a character in my play – you would wear those boots all the time.

SARAH. All the time?

EDMOND. I like those boots.

SARAH. What were you saying about a beard?

(She laughs at him. He thinks about kissing her.)

(They kiss.)

EDMOND. You are right. Hamlet is better with no beard.

(They kiss again as the scene shifts around them. He starts to undress her, and she him.)

Scene Two

(Sarah's dressing room.)

EDMOND. It is delightful to undress a man and find a woman inside.

SARAH. It is equally delightful to undress a man and find a man.

EDMOND. *(Kissing her.)* Glorious hair, beautiful breasts and...the altar of Venus.

SARAH. *(Laughing.)* Did you just say that?

EDMOND. Not me. Shakespeare.

SARAH. He didn't.

EDMOND. I'm sure he did. Didn't he?

SARAH. Well, as you are a poet yourself you may take credit for it.

EDMOND. Thank you, I think I shall.

SARAH. You were gone forever.

EDMOND. It's easier to write in the country.

SARAH. Away from me?

EDMOND. Yes, it is easier to write away from you as you are rather loud.

SARAH. Loud? Me?

EDMOND. I just mean you fill up a room.

SARAH. I'm an actress. I'm not much good if I don't.

EDMOND. The trees speak more quietly. The way they shift. All those subtle greens. The glint of water beyond. The house is nothing much! In the ceiling, enormous cracks, peeling paper, drapery so faded it nearly evaporates. But the world beyond speaks. If you listen. You and I, we live to pull from shadow to light, our dreams.

SARAH. What are you writing about?

EDMOND. It's but an early draft. I should not have returned, it's really not finished. But I could not stay away.

(He kisses her.)

SARAH. I'm coming with you next time.

EDMOND. That's a terrible idea.

SARAH. Why?

EDMOND. I won't get any work done.

SARAH. But I am your muse! You cannot live without me!

EDMOND. Yes you are, and no I cannot, which is why I came back.

SARAH. I want to see your play.

EDMOND. It's not ready and you already have a play. The mightiest of plays.

(*Then.*)

Why do you want to play him, Sarah?

SARAH. Oh why. Many are the male parts I should have liked to play. Mephistopheles. Tartuffe!

EDMOND. Then play them.

SARAH. Are you telling me not to play Hamlet?

EDMOND. No.

SARAH. Why shouldn't I play Hamlet. I am perfectly suited. Nobody cares about his masculinity. So-called. They care about the magnificent nuance of his heart.

EDMOND. Yes.

SARAH. His passion.

EDMOND. Yes.

SARAH. His joy.

EDMOND. His "joy"? He is the most miserable and melancholic of men!

SARAH. No one is going to come to the theater to see me play a depressed melancholic boy.

EDMOND. He is not a boy!

SARAH. I'm not going to argue with you about how old he is because I'm right. He is a passionate, confused boy with the mind of a man of forty. A young actor, of what, twenty cannot understand the philosophy of Hamlet. An older actor no longer looks the boy, nor has he the ready heart of the woman who can combine the light carriage of youth with the mature thought of the man.

The woman more readily looks the part and feels the
part, yet has the subtleness of mind to grasp it.

> *(Looks at him.)*

What?

EDMOND. Nothing. You are brilliant, and it is bold.

> *(He kisses her.)*
>
> *(There is a knock on the door.)*

SARAH. Go away.

> *(Another knock.)*

Go away!

> *(**LYSETTE** enters.)*

I'm sorry. Does "go away" now mean "barge in"?

LYSETTE. Very sorry, Madame Sarah. But there's a man at
the stage door.

SARAH. There are always men at the stage door. Tell him to
go away, I'm not here.

LYSETTE. He's not looking for you.

> *(There is a pause.)*

SARAH. Then why are you here?

LYSETTE. He is looking for Monsieur Rostand. He was sent
by his wife. He says to tell him that the baby is ill.

> *(There is an unhappy pause at this.)*

What should I tell him.

SARAH. Tell him to go away!

EDMOND. Tell him that you spoke with Madame Sarah who
says she saw me earlier today, and that I have gone to
dinner with friends at Le Voltigeur.

> *(**SARAH** falls back on the couch. **LYSETTE** curtsies
> and goes. **EDMOND** starts to dress himself.)*

SARAH. Your wife has sent a man to my dressing room
looking for you. I think we can safely say she suspects.

EDMOND. She knew I was coming here to watch the
rehearsal today.

SARAH. That was hours ago.

EDMOND. And I'm not here now.

SARAH. You know, for a man who was undressing another man mere moments ago, I would say you are acting very conventional.

EDMOND. The baby is sick.

SARAH. Babies are always sick! What, they are!

EDMOND. This from you.

SARAH. Yes, this is from me!

EDMOND. You know if you heard your son was sick you would –

SARAH. *(He's got her.)* All right. All right. I would fly to his side. But I'm a woman. I'm dramatic.

EDMOND. I must go.

SARAH. Leave her for me.

(This stops him for a moment.)

EDMOND. You have my heart and soul, why is that not enough?

SARAH. I know it should be but it just never is.

(They consider each other sadly for a moment, then he goes.)

Scene Three

*(**LOUIS** and **EDMOND** having a drink.)*

LOUIS. You have a new play.

EDMOND. It is not finished.

LOUIS. I should love to see it, when it is. An early preview, perhaps.

EDMOND. A critic's privilege?

LOUIS. Critic and friend; it is my hope we can be both.

EDMOND. Mine as well. I was so pleased to receive your invitation to join you for coffee.

LOUIS. You have risen to our attention. Your first two or three plays didn't quite get there but there's a sense that you will. People are interested. So tell me about this new one. It is for our Divine Sarah, of course.

EDMOND. It would be my honor, of course. But she is presently engaged.

LOUIS. Not another revival of Camille, I hope. She's a bit long in the tooth for it.

EDMOND. She is rehearsing Hamlet, actually.

LOUIS. Hamlet? Who is her Hamlet?

EDMOND. She...is her Hamlet.

LOUIS. I do not take your meaning.

EDMOND. She is playing Hamlet.

LOUIS. She is? Sarah Bernhardt? A woman. Playing Hamlet? You saw this?

EDMOND. A rehearsal.

LOUIS. Any good?

EDMOND. It was a rehearsal.

> *(He is getting irked now, and defensive on her behalf.)*

LOUIS. A woman playing Hamlet. Yes of course she can do it, but one does need to ask, why? What's the point.

EDMOND. It is the greatest part ever written and she the greatest actress ever born.

LOUIS. There are people who will argue that for you.

EDMOND. Not you, I hope.

LOUIS. Not I, of course not. She is our Divine Sarah, she is our queen! Getting a little old I suppose. Can't play Ophelia anymore. Why not Gertrude?

EDMOND. It's not much of a part.

LOUIS. It's not a bad part.

EDMOND. It's not Hamlet.

LOUIS. Can't she keep playing Camille? She dies so beautifully.

EDMOND. You just said...

LOUIS. Don't argue with me about this, you don't like it either.

EDMOND. I haven't said that.

LOUIS. You haven't said you do like it. So they're rehearsing it?

EDMOND. Yes.

LOUIS. To open when?

EDMOND. She didn't say.

LOUIS. I imagine she's rehearsing in breeches? I mean, she couldn't rehearse in a skirt, it'd make no sense.

EDMOND. She is using costume pieces for rehearsal.

LOUIS. So breeches. You've seen her legs then.

EDMOND. Yes. As have you.

LOUIS. Lorenzaccio, quite. Beautiful. Her legs.

(He thinks about that.)

EDMOND. You can come get a look at them again when she opens her Hamlet.

LOUIS. Someone needs to talk her out of it. She's a great actress, but Hamlet? It's grotesque. If Shakespeare meant for Hamlet to be a woman, he would have named the play Hamlet Princess of Denmark. That's not what he wrote.

EDMOND. The men played the women for all those years. If it's all right for a man to play a woman, why not a woman play a man?

LOUIS. It was the custom. Men playing women, that's all right. Women playing men. It doesn't work.

EDMOND. How do you know?

LOUIS. Don't argue with me about this. I've already won this argument. It's a disgusting idea and you know it.

EDMOND. "Disgusting"?

LOUIS. Most men will find it so. The women too! The women will be the worst. We accept all manner of eccentricity from her. Her fashion? I know many people admire it but there's no question, it's extreme. That bat hat. What is that? And all those lovers. You have to admit it's unseemly at best. And those pets. She actually kept a panther as a pet, that's not a rumor, I saw it! It scared the wits out of me. But here's my point. We accept all of it. This however –

EDMOND. Playing Hamlet is no eccentricity.

LOUIS. Don't be ridiculous of course it is. It's a gimmick. It's unnatural.

EDMOND. I disagree.

LOUIS. And you need her for your play!

EDMOND. My play is not finished and it is irrelevant.

LOUIS. A playwright who thinks his play is irrelevant, that's a new one.

EDMOND. You mistake my meaning.

LOUIS. What is your meaning?

EDMOND. I have no meaning other than my dedication to our greatest actress. She commands our loyalty.

LOUIS. Oh is that what she commands.

EDMOND. And now I do not take your meaning.

LOUIS. Oh don't you.

EDMOND. No I do not.

LOUIS. Oh now, you can't get offended because we all want to –

EDMOND. I am offended!

LOUIS. Why? She's not.

EDMOND. I beg your pardon. I am tired. The new baby is... it cries.

LOUIS. Does it?

EDMOND. A lot.

LOUIS. No one told you to have children.

(*Fed up finally,* **EDMOND** *stands.*)

Don't go, don't go. I'm teasing.

EDMOND. You are unpleasant.

LOUIS. How so? We're just talking about Sarah Bernhardt playing Hamlet.

EDMOND. You're not talking, you're attacking.

LOUIS. Not at all! Over and again I've acknowledged her genius. You are choosing to be intentionally obtuse.

EDMOND. I am not choosing. This manner of speaking so coldly about a great artist, an icon, even, as if she were just a toy to play with, it offends me deeply. She is not merely an actress. She is a reckoning of the soul.

LOUIS. A "reckoning"?

EDMOND. You may mock me for saying so but I know her, I've created with her, I love her.

(*Then.*)

As an artist she is my muse. I'm not the only one who would say so.

LOUIS. I apologize for offending your feelings. Sit sit please. It's a misunderstanding.

(**EDMOND** *sits.*)

EDMOND. My apologies. She is a lady I admire greatly. I cannot of course agree to hearing her attacked.

LOUIS. I am not attacking! I am contemplating. Madame Sarah is revered by all, why throw that in our faces?

Even if Hamlet were a woman you wouldn't want this woman playing him, her, him, her. She doesn't have the instrument. She is light, sensual, amusing.

EDMOND. You are deciding that you don't like it even before you've seen it.

LOUIS. Oh now. I'm a critic. We're paid to have opinions and then everyone gets angry when we do.

EDMOND. You are pedantic.

LOUIS. Are you sure that insulting me is the best way to defend this absurd whim of an aging actress?

(A beat.)

Forgive me. You know I adore her.

EDMOND. I do not doubt it. I apologize if I seemed abrupt.

LOUIS. You're hurt, on her behalf. Because you love her!

EDMOND. No. Well. Perhaps.

LOUIS. What are we arguing about? You and I agree. She can't play the ingénue anymore.

EDMOND. No one wants her to.

LOUIS. But do you want her to play Hamlet?

*(**EDMOND** doesn't answer.)*

(Blackout.)

Scene Four

(**SARAH**, *in light, the players around her.*)

SARAH. To be or not to be, that is the question.
  Whether 'tis nobler in the mind to suffer
  The slings and arrows of outrageous fortune,
  Or to take arms against a sea of troubles,
  And by opposing, end them.

  (Then.)

  I like that. To take arms. To stand up.

CONSTANT. There's different thoughts on that.

SARAH. Different how?

CONSTANT. To die, to sleep no more. Some think he means take arms and end his life.

SARAH. Take arms means take arms whether it is against himself or no.

  (Then.)

  To die, to sleep,
  No more, and by a sleep, to say we end
  The heartache and the thousand natural shocks
  That flesh is heir to. 'Tis a consummation
  Devoutly to be wished.

  (Then.)

  He's talking about sex again. He endlessly talks about sex, our Hamlet. And yet he never does anything about it.

LYSETTE. You don't think he and Ophelia have been going at it?

SARAH. They don't in the play.

CONSTANT. They could.

SARAH. I've played her three times and no one has ever even suggested it. She's a prop, mostly.

CONSTANT. You were never a prop.

SARAH. Well not me, but...she and Hamlet are going at it?

LYSETTE. They could.

>(**CONSTANT** *shrugs. He is eating a ham sandwich now.*)

SARAH. They could.

>(*She climbs onto* **LYSETTE**, *sexually aggressive.*)

Are you honest?

LYSETTE. Am I –

SARAH. Are you fair?

>(*She kisses her.*)

LYSETTE. What means your lordship?

>(**SARAH** *mounts her, starts to have sex... It is increasingly passionate between them.*)

SARAH. If you be honest and fair your honesty should admit no discourse to your beauty.

LYSETTE. Could beauty, my lord, have better commerce than with honesty?

SARAH. Ay truly; for the power of beauty will sooner transform honesty from what it is to be a bawd, than the force of honesty can translate beauty into his likeness: this was sometime a paradox, but now the time gives it proof.

>(*They are full-on having sex. They both come...*)

I did love you once.

LYSETTE. (*Recovering.*) Indeed my lord you made me believe so.

>(**SARAH** *considers that whole thing.*)

SARAH. That would certainly get their attention.

RAOUL. It got my attention.

CONSTANT. I like it. It doesn't really speak to the monologue.

SARAH. The monologue?

CONSTANT. To be or not to be.

SARAH. Oh, that monologue. It's endless. Some of it lovely. "To sleep, perchance to Dream, ay there's the rub, for in that sleep of death, what dreams may come, when we have shuffled off this mortal coil, must give us pause." I slept in a coffin precisely because I wanted to know the answer to that question.

LYSETTE. And what did you learn?

SARAH. Very comfortable. Cozy even.

LYSETTE. You really slept in it? That wasn't just for the photograph?

SARAH. I never do anything just for the photograph.

RAOUL. So it wasn't confining?

SARAH. It was completely confining.

RAOUL. I wouldn't like that. I like to spread.

SARAH. That's not really possible in a coffin.

FRANÇOIS. I liked that picture of you in there. You looked dead. I mean it. Really dead.

SARAH. I was acting.

FRANÇOIS. Obviously. But you weren't acting scared. Just – dead.

SARAH. You didn't think I was asleep?

FRANÇOIS. Were you?

SARAH. Not while they were taking the picture.

CONSTANT. Hamlet does the same thing. He jumps into the open grave, he grabs the dead body of his dead love.

FRANÇOIS. He doesn't love her.

CONSTANT. He does.

FRANÇOIS. No no no.

CONSTANT. You ever play him?

FRANÇOIS. I'm always the gravedigger.

CONSTANT. Then what do you know.

SARAH. Let's do that scene today. Raoul, can I have your rapier?

CONSTANT. We're doing the graveyard scene now?

SARAH. At least something happens in the graveyard scene. I cannot get inside these endless poems.

(Trying the words again.)

This mortal coil. Coil...coil? The meaning escapes. It has no music.

LYSETTE. What dreams may come.

SARAH. Yes, that's good.

LYSETTE. The sleep of death.

SARAH. I said some of it was very good. It just seems... inauthentic.

FRANÇOIS. Shakespeare?

SARAH. Anyone who writes as much as he did is bound to slip once in a while.

CONSTANT. But "To be or not to be"?

SARAH. All I'm saying is it's a bit formal and well argued. If you're thinking of killing yourself a little more desperation might be in order. It can begin as a well-reasoned argument but doesn't utter terror have a place? Doesn't it?

CONSTANT. You've never thought of killing yourself, then?

SARAH. Why kill yourself when there is so much to do?

CONSTANT. He's unhappy. Life is a burden to him.

SARAH. He has so much fun with the players. Maybe we should do that scene.

CONSTANT. He does, it's true. But he's stuck in his head, you know. For all that talk, he doesn't see the world as it is. "There is something in this more than natural if philosophy could find it out."

RAOUL. Sorry, you played him?

CONSTANT. *(And others.)* Four times.

Not in Paris, never in Paris. In the south mostly. I saw Irving do it. And Macready.

SARAH. If they can do it why not I?

CONSTANT. You'll get no argument from me. Particularly as you've given me a job. I like Polonius. He's a bit of a fool, but he has a good heart. Straight-ahead fellow, really. You play him, you go home, you go to bed.

SARAH. Not Hamlet.

CONSTANT. Oh god no. You play him, you go home, you're up all night. It's a cage really, his mind. That's what it feels like. Everywhere you turn, there's another problem.

SARAH. Yes!

CONSTANT. Beautiful words, but where do they take him?

SARAH. You don't think he's mad?

(A man enters at the back of the theater.)

CONSTANT. He'll drive you mad if you let him. It's a lot of words. He wrote it for Burbage, who apparently had a head for lines.

*(**SARAH** sees the newcomer, brightens.)*

SARAH. Alphonse!

ALPHONSE. Madame Sarah.

(The others greet him.)

Hello, hello. Constant. The beautiful Lysette, yes, hello.

*(He bows to **LYSETTE**.)*

LYSETTE. Monsieur Mucha.

SARAH. Lysette will share the stage with me as Ophelia, Constant will appear as her father, Polonius.

CONSTANT. And your father too.

(She looks at him, startled.)

SARAH. My father? What of him?

CONSTANT. The ghost.

SARAH. Yes, the ghost! Just so. Also the ghost.

*(Presenting herself to **ALPHONSE**.)*

This is the costume, what do you think?

ALPHONSE. Did you do it yourself?

SARAH. With advice from my fellow players.

CONSTANT. He's always in black. That was my only contribution.

ALPHONSE. I like your boots, they are good. Is there a rapier?

SARAH. Oh yes. A rapier we have. And capes,
(*To* **FRANÇOIS**.) could you ask Marcelline to send up three or four of the better choices, she knows what I like. Nothing from Lorenzaccio. And no hats.

ALPHONSE. Perhaps armor.

SARAH. Armor?

ALPHONSE. For the ghost.

CONSTANT. I'm to be on the poster?

SARAH. Of course, you must.

ALPHONSE. (*To* **LYSETTE**.) And flowers, yes, for the fair Ophelia.

SARAH. Brilliant. I am in your hands, my friend.

ALPHONSE. No Madame Sarah. We are all in yours.

SARAH. Raoul can you help them carry all that to the stage.

(*The players leave.* **ALPHONSE** *and* **SARAH** *are alone.*)

So tell me the truth, Alphonse. What do you think of my plan to play Hamlet?

ALPHONSE. You are a success in everything you touch, Madame Sarah.

SARAH. As are you.

(*She is restless. He sketches her as she moves about the stage. She picks up her rapier, makes a few moves with it.*)

Have you seen Edmond?

ALPHONSE. Rostand?

SARAH. Is there another? He's off to the country for god knows how long and then as soon as he returns he disappears again.
(*Immediate apology.*) I'm sorry. Forgive me. Two weeks can feel like a long time

ALPHONSE. There is nothing to forgive. You have begun a mighty work. It fills you, as it must.

SARAH. I am finding it trying, it must be confessed. I think of sending for Maurice. Who better to teach you how to play a youth of nineteen than your own son. Even if he is thirty-five.

ALPHONSE. You must send for him then.

SARAH. No no. He is at school. Even if he is thirty-five.

ALPHONSE. Just like Hamlet.

SARAH. Don't think I haven't marked the similarities. I want him to stay there and stay out of this.

(*He watches as she considers her rapier.*)

ALPHONSE. What are you afraid of?

SARAH. I am not afraid!

(*Then.*)

I am a little afraid.

ALPHONSE. A little fear can be the worst kind.

SARAH. Or the best. None is better yet.

ALPHONSE. (*Reminding her.*) It is not your first breeches part.

SARAH. I prefer the pants truth be told. It's easier by far to move about the stage. But Lorenzaccio is no comparison to this. Next to Hamlet he's one-note, a fop.

ALPHONSE. Lorenzo de Medici was no fop. At least not the way you played him.

SARAH. I cannot remember how I played him!

(*She slices the air with the rapier, impatient.*)

ALPHONSE. No please, can you sheath it, on your belt?

SARAH. Of course.

(*She does.*)

ALPHONSE. With voice, with gesture, with your hands, your body. You are as always a painting come alive.

SARAH. I know that sounds like a compliment, and it is a compliment, coming from you, Alphonse, but it does me no good with Hamlet. I am a celebrity. Hamlet is not.

ALPHONSE. He is the prince.

SARAH. Yes yes yes. That's not what I mean. He has stature, but he balks, he clings to thought. He hides in words words and more words. It's the whole point I'm told. Who wants to see that?

ALPHONSE. They don't come to see Hamlet. They come to see you be Hamlet.

SARAH. Well, if they don't come, I am quite finished.

ALPHONSE. Actors always say that.

SARAH. Sometimes they say it because it is true.

ALPHONSE. Finished. The Divine Sarah?

SARAH. I have no money. I have no money.

(He looks up at that, surprised. She nods.)

ALPHONSE. La Samaritaine was a tremendous success.

SARAH. With the critics. Audiences didn't want to see it. God help me, a gospel in verse in three tableaux, love filled the theater with a joy of infinite purity; I lost two million francs. The best thing about that was your poster.

ALPHONSE. Not so. Well. Maybe so.

SARAH. Rostand wrote it for me! And it was a disaster. No matter, he's a genius, he'll come up with something new. But I can't do this anymore in those small houses. I need more income, and I need space. I can't count on you to make me beautiful when the audiences are right on top of me. They see every wrinkle. I can no longer play the divinely dying Camille. It is an embarrassment.

ALPHONSE. You are ageless.

SARAH. No one is ageless. Least of all an actress.

ALPHONSE. Ridiculous.

SARAH. It's not ridiculous, I am too old to play her and what's more I don't want to do it. I have revived her so many times she is death personified. I cannot die every night anymore. I am simply done dying.

ALPHONSE. Hamlet dies.

SARAH. But he kills as well.

ALPHONSE. An actor's dream?

SARAH. An actress's, perhaps. We never get to kill anyone.

ALPHONSE. Medea.

SARAH. Oh well yes Medea. But she makes my point for me! She didn't want to kill her own children. She was furious with Jason. Women. All we ever get to do is sit around and mope for love. The power that eludes us.

ALPHONSE. Does power elude you?

SARAH. Well not me, maybe that's why Hamlet is driving me mad. All that privilege and he can't figure out how to do anything? A woman would never have got away with it.

ALPHONSE. Many women do nothing.

SARAH. And who cares about them? A woman who cannot do anything is nothing. A man who does nothing is Hamlet.

> *(He laughs.)*

You know I am right.

ALPHONSE. That's why I'm laughing.

CONSTANT. *(Ghastly, offstage.)* Swear.

SARAH. What? What is that?

> *(The door opens and **CONSTANT** enters in costume.)*

CONSTANT. It's me!

> *(Then.)*

Swear.

ALPHONSE. *(Taken.)* Beautiful.

SARAH. Constant is always very good.

> *(**LYSETTE** enters with flowers, **RAOUL** carrying capes.)*

ALPHONSE. We have the cape, yes?

RAOUL. They sent up several.

ALPHONSE. This one I think.

LYSETTE. There's rosemary, that's for remembrance. Pray you, love, remember. And there is pansies, that's for thoughts.

RAOUL. A document in madness. Thoughts and remembrance fitted.

LYSETTE. There's fennel for you, and columbines. There's rue for you...

ALPHONSE. I don't need the lines. You're perfect as-is. Here, let's put you here. Madame Sarah, you over there.

> (*He drapes the cape around* **SARAH** *and constructs the stage picture until it presents as a tableau of the famous poster.*)
>
> (*Blackout.*)

Scene Five

(A Paris street. **EDMOND** *looks at the La Samaritaine poster, which is torn but still glorious. A* **WORKER** *approaches, about to take it down.* **ALPHONSE** *approaches with his sketchbook.)*

ALPHONSE. Leave it please, please leave it.

WORKER. The show's closed.

ALPHONSE. And when the next is coming in, you may take this one. But since I am the one who is designing the new poster I happen to know you don't have it because I haven't finished it. So this one can stay.

WORKER. There's no reason to leave it up.

ALPHONSE. It's beautiful, that's the reason.

WORKER. Won't sell any tickets.

ALPHONSE. It's beautiful!

WORKER. It's got to come down eventually.

ALPHONSE. Yes yes. Art versus commerce is a truly fascinating debate. But go away. Go away!

(The **WORKER** *goes.* **EDMOND** *watches* **ALPHONSE** *sketch.)*

EDMOND. So she's doing it.

ALPHONSE. Did you think she would change her mind?

EDMOND. I don't think about it.

ALPHONSE. No?

EDMOND. No.

ALPHONSE. All of Paris is talking about it, and you don't think of it, or her. Curious.

EDMOND. She has been known to change her mind.

ALPHONSE. Not this time. She has to do something. La Samaritaine was an utter failure. She lost millions on it.

EDMOND. It was a critical triumph.

ALPHONSE. Which is absolutely what she tells her creditors. What are you yelling at me about, it was a critical triumph. As they cart off her furniture. I didn't need furniture anyway, it was a critical triumph. As they repossess her gowns –

EDMOND. Enough.

ALPHONSE. It matters not that I am left in my underwear! It was a critical triumph!

EDMOND. You are as histrionic as she.

ALPHONSE. Histrionic. Is not a kind word.

EDMOND. My apologies. It is never my intent to be ingracious.

ALPHONSE. You look terrible. You look like you haven't slept in a week.

EDMOND. Closer to two.

ALPHONSE. Sarah says she hasn't seen you.

EDMOND. I went as soon as I was back in the city.

ALPHONSE. Since then.

EDMOND. I have a baby. I have a play. I have a wife.

ALPHONSE. I'm not going to go back and tell her that.

EDMOND. Oh please.

ALPHONSE. Why will you not go see her? She is asking for you, she needs you!

EDMOND. *(Flaring.)* You cannot pretend this is a simple situation. This is not – a small thing, it's not a dalliance. It's a catastrophe. I have to stay away and you know it.

ALPHONSE. What does it matter to stay away if all you can then do is wander around the streets of Paris, looking at pictures of her?

EDMOND. Would you deny me this small comfort? To see her, in your beautiful visions of her?

(They look at the poster.)

ALPHONSE. La Samaritaine. I prefer it of all of them. She is so graceful, at peace. Angelic even. You allowed her to be a Jew. I think it made her happy. I don't know about Hamlet.

(To **EDMOND.***)* The poster. Not the play.

EDMOND. I took your meaning.

ALPHONSE. Rostand. You are in love with her, of course, what of it? We all are.

EDMOND. She lives inside me. She lives inside my words. She is everywhere, in my sleep, in my dreams, in my daydreams, in the air, in the moon, the owl, the laughter of my children. Everything brings me to her. When I am with her, the reality of her – sometimes, I am afraid it makes everything else impossible. My whole life becomes impossible.

ALPHONSE. Love is always a predicament.

EDMOND. Oh thank you.

ALPHONSE. I mean it is! And she – well – if love is a predicament, loving her is perhaps... I cannot say what it might be. Beyond...

EDMOND. Yes.

(He cannot say more than that. **ALPHONSE** *nods, with some compassion.)*

ALPHONSE. *(Off poster.)* So easy to make her beautiful. Medea! The floating dead children at her feet, a dagger in her hand, you couldn't do it, couldn't even attempt it if she didn't command the whole composition with those haunted eyes. Gismonda, who cared what the play was about, the name is pretty and she is glorious. Lorenzaccio even, she calls him a fop, which is ridiculous, he was no fop, she was just so sensuous in that costume. Hamlet, of course, is impossible. The ghost of the dead father takes over everything. Ophelia, beauty, madness, flowers, perfection, that's good, but she's a subplot. What is Hamlet? Who can say. Her hair looks terrible.

EDMOND. You mean his hair.

ALPHONSE. You would say that, but you can't. Do you like it?

EDMOND. No.

ALPHONSE. No, don't spare my feelings.

EDMOND. You just told me you didn't like it!

ALPHONSE. That's different.

(Remembering it.) La Dame aux Camélias, completely rapturous, the thing painted itself. If only we could have her die for us forever.

(Blackout.)

Scene Six

*(The stage. The ghost above, **SARAH** below,
with **RAOUL** and **FRANÇOIS**, terrified.)*

SARAH. Angels and ministers of grace defend us!
    Be thou a spirit of health or goblin damn'd,
    Bring with thee airs from heaven or blasts from hell,
    Be thy intents wicked or charitable,
    Thou comest in such a questionable shape
    That I will speak to thee: I'll call thee Hamlet,
    King, father, royal Dane: O answer me!
    Let me not burst in ignorance; but tell
    Why thy canonized bones, hearsed in death,
    Have burst their cerements; why the sepulchre,
    Wherein we saw thee quietly inurn'd,
    Hath oped his ponderous and marble jaws,
    To cast thee up again. What may this mean,
    That thou, dead corse, again in complete steel
    Revisit'st thus the glimpses of the moon,
    Making night hideous; and we fools of nature
    So horridly to shake our disposition
    With thoughts beyond the reaches of our souls?
    Say, why is this? Wherefore? What should we do?

      *(The ghost beckons. The ghost beckons again.
      A beat.)*

    Is that me? That can't be me. God I can't believe there's
    more to that.

FRANÇOIS. No sorry, it's me, it's me. "Look, with what
    courteous action."

CONSTANT. No, no no.

RAOUL. Oh sorry, it's me.

      (Then.)

    It beckons you to go away with it,
    As if it some impartment did desire to you alone.

(There is another pause.)

SARAH. Is that me?

FRANÇOIS. Oh sorry, it's me. "Look with what courteous action It waves you to a more removed ground: But do not go with it."

SARAH. It will not speak, then I will follow it.

RAOUL. No sorry that's me.

SARAH. Oh and it was going so well. Where are the pages?

> *(**CONSTANT** digs them out and shows them to her. She studies the lines.)*

RAOUL. I think I should be downstage.

FRANÇOIS. How about this?

> *(He throws himself on the ground and starts to crawl backwards. **SARAH** laughs at him.)*

SARAH. That's good, when's that?

FRANÇOIS. Top of the speech.

SARAH. Back that far?

FRANÇOIS. Look, my lord it comes!

RAOUL. That's my line.

FRANÇOIS. That's what I mean, you say it –

RAOUL. Where am I –

CONSTANT. Where am I?

FRANÇOIS. You're not on yet.

SARAH. Just show it.

FRANÇOIS. You're off! You're off. And then you come on.

> *(**CONSTANT** goes. They all look at each other.)*

CONSTANT. *(Offstage.)* So what's the cue?

FRANÇOIS. The same cue!

CONSTANT. *(Offstage.)* Just making sure.

> *(The three left onstage look at each other. **FRANÇOIS** drifts away, looking about, as **SARAH** speaks to **RAOUL**.)*

SARAH. So I'll just take it from –

Angels and ministers of grace defend us!
Be thou a spirit of health or goblin damn'd,
Bring with thee airs from heaven or blasts from hell.

RAOUL. Look, my lord, it comes!

(*The ghost appears.* **FRANÇOIS** *sees it, drops to his knees, and backs away, terrified. They all stop.* **SARAH** *looks at* **FRANÇOIS**.)

SARAH. That's very good.

FRANÇOIS. Thank you.

SARAH. You are going to have to get under it a little more. If you want the audience to feel it, you have to feel it. Constant, can we bump ahead to the next scene? I wanted to look at the orchard speech.

CONSTANT. Oh you want to?

SARAH. I think we must. It will give Marcellus and Horatio a chance to learn their lines.

(**RAOUL** *and* **FRANÇOIS** *go upstage to run lines.*)

CONSTANT. From where do you want to take it?

SARAH. Murder most foul? You were...

CONSTANT. I was downstage of you but for this moment that didn't feel quite right –

SARAH. It didn't, did it?

CONSTANT. What if I go up and come down, and then you counter.

SARAH. Let's try it.

CONSTANT. Murder most foul; as in the best it is:
But 'tis most foul, strange, and unnatural.

SARAH. Haste me to know't that I, with wings as swift
As meditation or the thoughts of love,
May sweep to my revenge.

CONSTANT. I find thee apt;
And duller should'st thou be than the fat weed
That roots itself in ease on Lethe wharf

Wouldst thou not stir in this. Now Hamlet, hear;
'Tis given out that, sleeping in mine orchard,
A serpent stung me; but know, thou noble youth,
The serpent that did sting thy father's life,
Now wears his crown.

SARAH. O my prophetic soul! Mine uncle!

> (**CONSTANT** *continues in the grand style of the late nineteenth century. It is rather bombastic.*)

CONSTANT. Ay, that incestuous, that adulterate beast,
With witchcraft of his wit, with traitorous gifts,
Won to his shameful lust
The will of my most seeming-virtuous queen:
O Hamlet, what a falling-off was there!
From me, whose love was that of dignity
That it went hand in hand even with the vow
I made to her in marriage, and to decline
Upon a wretch whose natural gifts were poor
To those of mine!
But virtue, as it never will be moved,
Though Lewdness court it in a shape of heaven,
So Lust though to a radiant angel linked –

> (*He sees that* **SARAH**, **RAOUL**, *and* **FRANÇOIS** *are laughing at this.*)

(*Dry.*) Do you want me to keep going?

SARAH. There's more?

CONSTANT. Quite a bit, I'm afraid.

> (*He again pulls pages out of his costume, shows them to her.*)

SARAH. How much of it do we need? I like the hell part.

CONSTANT. Well, that's the good stuff.

SARAH. We'll leave that as-is. But the rest is exposition, isn't it? Everyone knows the story. My audience is not coming to the theater to see me stand there and listen to a ghost.

CONSTANT. You do it well.

SARAH. Why don't I care? It's not unnerving. I'm not feeling it.

CONSTANT. Do you want me to ooooooo?

(*He makes a ghost sound and gesture.*)

SARAH. No, no. He comes in wearing all that armor. Why does he come in armor? I'm his son. Why doesn't he just talk to me?

CONSTANT. I did it four times and I never thought about it that way.

SARAH. Give me a minute. Let's try something.

(*She turns to him, urgent.*)

Why did you abandon me?

CONSTANT. What? Because I was murdered!

SARAH. No, no come with me on this.

CONSTANT. Oh. Ohhh...no...

(*He hates this stuff. She encourages him.*)

SARAH. You were never here. You held me away from you. There was nothing but silence between us. I didn't know you at all, ever.

(*She is fierce, dramatic, and very good.*)

CONSTANT. I'm here now, aren't I?

SARAH. Because you want to use me! You didn't come for me!

CONSTANT. You're right. No matter, my love for you. I am the king!

SARAH. You were the king! Now you're nothing. You're just dead!

CONSTANT. (*Fierce in return.*) That's right. But even from the nether reaches of hell, king I remain to my son if to no one else. Am I not your father?

SARAH. (*An admission.*) Very like.

(**CONSTANT** *falls into the authenticity of the acting.*)

CONSTANT. I am thy father's spirit;
Doomed for a certain term to walk the night,
And for the day confined to fast in fires,
'Til the foul crimes done in my days of nature
Are burnt and purged away. But that I am forbid
To tell the secrets of my prison-house,
I could a tale unfold, whose lightest word
Would harrow up thy soul; freeze thy young blood;
Make thy two eyes, like stars, start from their spheres;
Thy knotted and combined locks to part,
And each particular hair to stand on end,
Like quills upon the fretful porcupine,
But 'tis eternal blazon must not be
To ears of flesh and blood. List, list, O, list!
If thou didst ever thy dear father love.

SARAH. Oh god!

CONSTANT. Revenge his foul and most unnatural murder.

SARAH. Murder?

CONSTANT. Murder most foul; as in the best it is:
But 'tis most foul, strange, and unnatural.

SARAH. Haste me to know't that I, with wings as swift
As meditation or the thoughts of love,
May sweep to my revenge.

CONSTANT. Adieu! Adieu! Remember me! Remember me!

(He goes. **SARAH** *is broken-hearted.)*

SARAH. Remember thee?
Ay thou poor ghost, whiles memory holds a seat
In this distracted globe. Yes, by heaven!
O most pernicious woman!
O villain, villain, smiling, damned villain!
Remember thee?

*(***CONSTANT*** watches this, transfixed. She looks at him.)*

CONSTANT. I think there's something there.

SARAH. Fathers are ephemeral things.

CONSTANT. That's why he's a ghost.

SARAH. My own father was a ghost. Nowhere near this amusing. He just...didn't exist. Hamlet is lucky by comparison. In any event, I think the cut is a terrific idea. It's far too many lines. I don't know how you remember them all.

CONSTANT. Oh. It's the iamb.

SARAH. Please don't.

CONSTANT. Ba BA ba BA ba BA –

SARAH. *(Overlapping.)* Stop it.

CONSTANT. Ba BA.

SARAH. I know I know I know.

CONSTANT. Seriously, when you can't remember the lines, the poetry is all you've got.

SARAH. It doesn't always work like that.

CONSTANT. Ba BA ba BA ba BA.

SARAH. Yes yes yes yes yes, stop! Enough poetry and enough ghosts. I'm done for the day.

CONSTANT. *(Laughing as he leaves.)* Ba BA ba BA ba BA.

(He is gone. LYSETTE considers SARAH.)

LYSETTE. It doesn't always work like that.

SARAH. We'd all kill ourselves if it did. It intrudes. On the sense. It gets in the way, all that ba Ba ba Ba, of course not for Ophelia, she doesn't have to do it as much. Just a few times with Laertes and Polonius and you can justify that, she hides herself in the verse.

LYSETTE. I saw your Ophelia. You were heartbreaking. It makes me nervous, sometimes, to do the scenes. I think you must be watching me and thinking I'm so terrible.

SARAH. I'm not thinking about it honestly; Hamlet takes up a lot of room in my head. I'm sorry. No, you're very good. Lovely. And that dress – is that your costume?

LYSETTE. It doesn't have to be.

SARAH. The silhouette is charming but the color's not quite right, is it? We'll see what else we have in stock.

LYSETTE. Now?

SARAH. Tomorrow morning is fine.

LYSETTE. Well, good night.

(She starts to go again.)

SARAH. *(Defensive.)* I am not wrong to do this.

*(**LYSETTE** stops, turns.)*

LYSETTE. You are not wrong to do anything.

SARAH. Please don't agree with me just because I'm me. That gets – tiring.

LYSETTE. Does it?

SARAH. You'd be surprised.

LYSETTE. Sarah. We are grateful for what you do. If not you, then who? Then no one.

SARAH. The women are whispering against me. I hear it. Through the walls.

LYSETTE. Envy is the failing of the weak, you know that. It is their only power.

SARAH. It is, and they use it. Marcelline and her minions in the costume shop go silent as soon as I show up and shoot daggers at me with their eyes, as soon as my back is turned. You'd think I was the devil incarnate. Not him. Lilith, his succubus sister. Why do you think I send everyone else down there, she wears me out. I tell you, I'm tired.

LYSETTE. Then be tired.

SARAH. Do not interrupt me. I am tired and – oh god. I am just tired!

*(She looks at **LYSETTE**, expects an answer. **LYSETTE** just looks at her.)*

(Thinking.) I must always be strong. But Hamlet is not strong.

LYSETTE. He forces himself to be strong.

SARAH. So what? I must force myself to be weak so that then out of weakness I can force myself to be strong? It is too much, they ask too much of me. Maybe that's why women never try this. Who in her right mind would take her strength and then force it into weakness?

LYSETTE. Why do you doubt yourself?

> (SARAH *cannot bring herself to answer that.* LYSETTE *nods.)*

He'll come back.

SARAH. What if he doesn't?

LYSETTE. If he doesn't, there are many who love you, Madame Sarah.

> (*She goes to* SARAH *and holds her.* SARAH *allows herself a moment of rest.*)

> (EDMOND *enters.*)

SARAH. Thank you, Lysette. You were wonderful today.

LYSETTE. Thank you.

> (*A nod to* EDMOND.)

Monsieur.

> (*She bows and exits.*)

EDMOND. Stopping early. You will never conquer Hamlet this way.

SARAH. We were doing the ghost scene. It took a toll. The ghost's speech, describing his own murder.

EDMOND. I know it well.

> (*The mood shifts. They are happy to see each other.*)

SARAH. Then you also know it goes on and on and on. And on.

EDMOND. It is considered lengthy.

SARAH. Here is my thought: He tells Hamlet that his own mother is the culprit.

EDMOND. Is she, though?

SARAH. She is implicated!

EDMOND. You are in a merry mood today.

SARAH. I wasn't, but I am. I am happy to see you.

EDMOND. I saw Alphonse on the street. He showed me sketches of the poster. They were good.

SARAH. Good but not great.

EDMOND. All of his posters of you are memorable.

SARAH. This one is not. At least not yet. I hate it. He has me looking, where am I looking? Where are my eyes? Where is Hamlet? The best part is the ghost, and Ophelia.

EDMOND. Not so.

SARAH. My hair looks terrible.

EDMOND. You are playing a man.

SARAH. I am inhabiting a man. He is the one who is playing. He plays with everyone.

It might not be him who is playing with us. It might be Shakespeare.

Why have you stayed away?

EDMOND. The baby has been ill. Colic, they call it. He screams incessantly. My wife needs all the help she can get.

SARAH. That's what servants are for.

EDMOND. We have let our servant go.

SARAH. *(A sudden shift, worried.)* Why have you let your servant go? Do you need money?

EDMOND. No, no.

SARAH. I can give you money.

EDMOND. I don't want your money, and Alphonse informs me you don't have any. Again.

SARAH. You were never paid for La Samaritaine.

EDMOND. No one was paid! No one came to see it!

SARAH. They came! Just not as many as we hoped for.

EDMOND. I will not take your money.

SARAH. You cannot even keep your servant!

EDMOND. She was domineering. Rosamond disliked her.

> *(This came out a little too unconsciously. His wife's appearance in the conversation does no one any favors.)*

SARAH. I would have wished that your wife had a less romantic name. Rosamond. Every time you say it, I can hear your yearning to love her.

EDMOND. It is not yearning that you hear.

SARAH. Good.

EDMOND. You know my meaning.

SARAH. I do not know your meaning. Your meaning is as usual elusive. Much like the rest of you.

EDMOND. Sarah.

SARAH. I will not let you speak another word in that tone. Come to my dressing room. We will talk.

EDMOND. Oh is that what we'll do.

(She goes to him, kisses him. He returns the kiss. They hold each other, then he looks around to make sure they are not seen.)

SARAH. No one is here.

EDMOND. We are on a stage! Everyone is here.

(He take a step away from her. She looks away.)

SARAH. Including your wife.

EDMOND. "Everyone" includes everyone.

SARAH. Why don't you leave her?

EDMOND. Why don't you leave the stage?

SARAH. Impossible.

EDMOND. Agreed. I love my wife and would not hurt her as you propose.

SARAH. Then why are you here?

EDMOND. I am here because Alphonse told me you had asked after me.

SARAH. You came for Alphonse. How flattering.

EDMOND. And because I am worried.

SARAH. Worried? About what?

EDMOND. The knives are poised for you, Sarah.

SARAH. What knives?

EDMOND. Our friends the critics. They find the idea of your Hamlet – problematic.

SARAH. Oh do they.

EDMOND. Surely you knew this would provoke.

SARAH. Actors play Hamlet all the time. Not all actors. Only the insane ones, you truly have to be mad as a hatter to take this on.

EDMOND. Women do not take it on.

SARAH. I take it on.

EDMOND. That's my point as you well know. You are Sarah Bernhardt. The eyes of the world are on you and you are once again doing something no other woman dares to do and this time you're not just putting on a funny hat or parading around with a pet panther. Hamlet is sacred to these men who may not be amused by your whim.

SARAH. "Whim."

EDMOND. That is how they see it.

(She looks at him, sharp.)

SARAH. That is why you come? To poison me?

EDMOND. No.

SARAH. To reach into my heart and tease any whisper of doubt into a raging terror –

EDMOND. I only wanted to warn you –

SARAH. I need no warnings. If I had heeded any warning in my whole life, I'd have done nothing with it. I want no warnings!

(A beat.)

I'm sorry. I can't hear doubt right now, I'm swimming in it. Of course, of course this is who Hamlet is, the uncertainty, the relentlessness of it – especially in rehearsal going over and over, all that inaction, it's worse than a bore, and then of course there he is, the ghost of your father! His murderous rage, come from where? Where is it that fathers go? Not to the afterworld. No. I'm not afraid of death, nor is Hamlet, honestly, he's afraid merely of the night, the panic of the soul, the terrifying dread of meaninglessness. Gone in the light of day, but at night it is nothing but the most malicious of battles, sanity is at risk, at night and that is finally where Hamlet puts himself. Turning a saint into a murderer is no mean trick.

EDMOND. Sarah –

SARAH. *(Angry now.)* What was I supposed to do? Take a final bow, as Camille, silent, charming, graceful. And then exit stage left. Farewell, farewell. Or dwindle into the benevolent Gertrude? That's a trick question, don't answer it. How may times wafting through this play as Ophelia. Hamlet is Shakespeare himself, you know he is. It is why every actor hungers after him, finally, because we are convinced this is how you know him, soul to soul, but within this web of words what if he is nothing but annihilation? If they demean it. If they demean me. I can't. Honestly I can't even...please, go.

EDMOND. I won't.

SARAH. You cannot stay if you merely come here to frighten me. I'm already out of my wits!

EDMOND. That is not why I'm here.

SARAH. Why are you here?

EDMOND. I am here because I cannot seem to survive away from you. I told myself I could, I must, I can live on memory, I can hoard the smell of you in a handkerchief I stole from your boudoir six months ago, sorry, I can read and read again the words I wrote for you, and your voice is there but it is an echo, or worse, a fabrication. It is not you. It is only a dream of you, and I am not alive, anywhere. Anywhere but here! I cannot separate what you are and what I am one from the other anymore. How many times have I watched you, standing out here alone knowing that it is my words you say, while they are hanging on your lips and your looks, it is my heart beating, it is my will, and soul, it is I who have taken years of my life to write our masterpiece only to disappear into the silence behind you.

SARAH. You never disappear.

EDMOND. Away from you, I do. I am nothing; I am a wraith in a dark wind. The only time I am fully alive is when I see you here, on the stage, launching yourself into eternity. But then it all comes back, my life, life itself, comes, in a rush that is so powerful I fear it might destroy me. And yet, there is no place for me here now. I cannot, I cannot be a part of any of this.

SARAH. Wait. Do you think I'm cheating on you with Shakespeare?

EDMOND. You know full well that you are not the one who's cheating.

SARAH. Edmond. It's the theater. Everybody cheats.

EDMOND. And lives are destroyed.

SARAH. But then why come at all? You had your escape. If that was what you wanted.

EDMOND. I do not know what I want, beyond the wanting of you. What is a playwright, what are words, without a voice? What am I, without you? Before you, what was I? I did not come here to frighten you. Frighten you? You fear nothing.

SARAH. I fear absence. I fear the absence of you.

(*A beat.*)

EDMOND. Doubt thou the stars are fire; Doubt that the sun doth move; Doubt truth to be a liar; But never doubt I love.

SARAH. Oh my god. He is crazy when he says that, you know, or insincere. No one knows what Hamlet means, that is a declaration of love, he isn't even the one who says it! Polonius reads it, it is corrupted from start to finish.

EDMOND. (*Overlapping.*) Sarah. Sarah.

(*He goes to her and kisses her to shut her up.*)

SARAH. You are just kissing me now, to shut me up.

EDMOND. Would that it worked.

SARAH. It works.

(They kiss again.)

EDMOND. Tell me about Hamlet.

SARAH. He is not easy. He is quicksand, our Hamlet. And I must say I have needed you. I cannot force myself into this morass without a hand, a soul, steadying.

EDMOND. You are surrounded –

SARAH. I do not want to be surrounded. I need – I need – there is something I need that is not just a whining woman wanting to be told a man loves her.

EDMOND. Tell me.

(She goes to him.)

SARAH. It is nothing. A small thing. But Edmond I tell you truly, only you can do it. Your brilliance, your wit, your tender heart. I cannot do this without you, Edmond. Truly I cannot.

EDMOND. I am at your command. You have slain me quite. What is it you would have me do?

SARAH. I want you to rewrite Hamlet.

(A beat.)

EDMOND. *(Pissed.)* You want me to rewrite Hamlet?

(Blackout.)

ACT TWO

Scene One

(The stage.)

*(***SARAH, RAOUL,*** *and* ***FRANÇOIS.****)*

FRANÇOIS. My honored lord.

RAOUL. My most dear lord.

SARAH. How dost thou, Guildenstern? Ah, Rosencrantz! Good lads! What's the news?

RAOUL. None, my lord, but that the world's grown honest.

SARAH. Then is doomsday near: but your news is not true. Let me question more in particular: what have you, my good friends, deserved at the hands of Fortune that she sends you to prison hither?

FRANÇOIS. Prison, my lord?

SARAH. Denmark's a prison.

RAOUL. Then is the world one.

SARAH. A goodly one, in which there are many confines, wards, and dungeons, Denmark being one of the worst.

RAOUL. We think not so, my lord.

SARAH. Why then 'tis none to you: for there is nothing either good or bad, but thinking makes it so: to me it is a prison.

RAOUL. Why, then, your ambition makes it one: 'tis too narrow for your mind.

SARAH. Oh god, I could be bounded in a nutshell and count myself a king of infinite space – were it not that I have bad dreams. Shall we to the court?

RAOUL & FRANÇOIS. We shall wait upon you.

SARAH. No such matter, I will not sort you with the rest of my servants, for to speak to you like an honest man, I am most dreadfully attended. But in the beaten way of friendship, what make you at Elsinore?

RAOUL. To visit you my lord; no other occasion.

SARAH. Were you not sent for? Is it a free visitation? Come, deal justly with me.

FRANÇOIS. What should we say my lord?

(They look at each other, uncomfortable.)

SARAH. Anything but to th' purpose. There is confession in your looks! I know the good queen and king have sent for you.

RAOUL. To what end, my lord?

SARAH. That you must teach me.

FRANÇOIS. My lord, we were sent for.

SARAH. I will tell you why. So shall my anticipation prevent your discovery, and your secrecy to the king and queen moult no feather. I have of late – but wherefore I know not – lost all my mirth, for gone all custom of exercises; and indeed it goes so heavily with my disposition that this goodly frame, the earth, seems to me a sterile promontory; this most excellent canopy, the air, look you – this brave o'erhanging firmament, this majestical roof fretted with golden fire, why it appears no other thing to me than a foul and pestilent congregation of vapors. What a piece of work is a man! How noble in reason! How infinite in faculty! In form and moving how express and admirable! In action how like an angel! In apprehension, how like a god! The beauty of the world and paragon of animals. And yet, to me, what is this quintessence of dust? Man delights not me; no, nor woman neither, though by your smiling you seem to say so.

(A beat. They are lost.)

Well?

RAOUL. Well?

SARAH. Well?

FRANÇOIS. That was good.

SARAH. *(Frustrated now.)* Good, I don't want to be good!

FRANÇOIS. Very good. No, I mean it. Very very good.

RAOUL. It was great. The cuts work well. And – that was great.

(**SARAH** *turns and looks at* **ALPHONSE**, *who watches.)*

SARAH. Well?

ALPHONSE. *(At a loss, but trying.)* I sketch. You live. Inside something so enormous, and when it rises in you, you transform us all. It is impossible to tell you what we see, when we watch you.

FRANÇOIS. That's what I meant.

RAOUL. You want to run it again?

SARAH. No. Thank you. Let's move on.

(**RAOUL** *and* **FRANÇOIS** *go.)*

ALPHONSE. I don't know how you do what you do.

(**SARAH** *thinks about that, disturbed and even annoyed.)*

SARAH. Neither do I.

ALPHONSE. Another triumph.

SARAH. I pray.

ALPHONSE. You "pray"? To whom?

SARAH. To the gods of theater. I don't know how to do it.

ALPHONSE. That was breathtaking.

SARAH. It's what they said of Keane. He couldn't do it all the time. Just in flashes. I cannot – stay there.

ALPHONSE. Sarah, that was truly beautiful.

SARAH. It's the prose part. It's easier.

ALPHONSE. You make light of your own majesty.

SARAH. I don't want to talk about it. Let me see.

(She looks at what he has sketched.)

SARAH. Oh god.

> *(She flips through his sketchbook.)*

Oh god.

> *(Another flip.)*

Oh god. My hair.

ALPHONSE. I know!

> **(SARAH** *stalks off.* **ALPHONSE** *stands, unhappy, considering his sketches.)*

Scene Two

(Lights shift to Edmond's study. **ALPHONSE** *enters, slams a bottle of Becherovka on the table, and starts to pour.)*

EDMOND. What's that?

ALPHONSE. It's Becherovka. Just drink it.

(He hands **EDMOND** *a drink. They both down it.)*

EDMOND. How is she?

ALPHONSE. She is unhappy, as she should be. The poster is terrible. I'm giving it up. I'm going to end my days designing those ridiculous little biscuit tins. It's all I'm fit for.

EDMOND. No no no no. The Divine Sarah is touching greatness again, there must be a poster to commemorate it.

(He goes and picks up the sketchbook, looks at it. Looks at **ALPHONSE.**)

ALPHONSE. I know! There is nothing there! Nothing.

(Then.)

I don't mean she is not good. She is very good. She is divine. She is light.

EDMOND. She is, yes.

ALPHONSE. Hamlet is not light.

(There is a pause at the sad truth of that.)

She finds him then she loses him.

EDMOND. Yet.

ALPHONSE. Yet she is great, I know. Yet we must stand by her, I know. Yet yet yet.

EDMOND. I meant she has not found him "yet."

ALPHONSE. Well I haven't found him either. More the point I haven't found her. God knows it's not that she cannot fill the tragedy, you saw her Medea. But perhaps she cannot fill HIS tragedy.

EDMOND. Is he tragic?

ALPHONSE. He dies! He goes mad and dies!

EDMOND. Is he mad?

ALPHONSE. Oh my god not you too. Here. Drink more, you need it. What is this? Your new play? What is it?

> *(He hands* **EDMOND** *the bottle and looks at the pages.* **EDMOND** *drinks.)*

EDMOND. It is...nothing.

ALPHONSE. It's Hamlet.

> *(Reading.)*

It's not Hamlet. What is it?

EDMOND. It is Hamlet without the poetry.

> *(He is unhappy.* **ALPHONSE** *keeps reading.)*

ALPHONSE. Why are you doing this?

EDMOND. Why do you think? She has demanded it of me.

ALPHONSE. She wants to do Hamlet without Hamlet.

EDMOND. She wants to do Hamlet without the poetry!

ALPHONSE. Then it's not Hamlet.

EDMOND. I have told her that.

ALPHONSE. And yet.

EDMOND. Have you ever tried saying no to her?

ALPHONSE. I try, yes I try all the time.

EDMOND. You do not.

ALPHONSE. I try a little.

> *(Reading.)*

It's not bad.

EDMOND. Oh my god.

ALPHONSE. I'm complimenting your writing. You're a wonderful writer. Rewriting Hamlet is not something I'd wish on many people.

EDMOND. Do you wish it on me?

ALPHONSE. Well, I don't pity you for it. It can't be worse than La Samaritaine... Oh sorry. Sorry.

EDMOND. The critics loved it.

ALPHONSE. Well then what do I know. The poster certainly came out well.

(He keeps reading the pages.)

Hamlet without the poetry. It's a little like Becherovka without the alcohol.

EDMOND. That's not what it's like. Why not put a stake in my heart.

ALPHONSE. So strange. No ba Ba ba Ba…

EDMOND. She says that's what she wants, that she can't make sense of the poetry but it is not possible that she does not understand the poetry, she is the most poetic of women!

ALPHONSE. But is she the most poetic of men?

EDMOND. Is poetry different in men and women?

ALPHONSE. Is it not?

EDMOND. I am not interested in the distinction.

ALPHONSE. Really? I am. The questions she raises. I've drawn her a hundred times, more than a hundred; she is always magnificent. But not as a man.

EDMOND. Lorenzaccio.

ALPHONSE. He doesn't count. He's a fop.

EDMOND. Lorenzo de Medici?

ALPHONSE. Listen to me. I never draw men! It is not my interest. I paint women endlessly and make them all look like flowers. But what if that is not what they are? No. Some of them have to be, at least some of the time, otherwise there is no explanation for my astonishing success. If they are not in essence the flower inside the self then what are they? I don't want to say this quest of hers is fraudulent. But perhaps it is mistaken? The self exposed. Is the female self exposed essentially the same as the male self exposed? I'm just going to say it. She has no penis. But then neither does Hamlet really.

EDMOND. I'm not having this conversation.

ALPHONSE. You can't escape it. This question of Hamlet is beyond us all. And if he is beyond men, is he not more so beyond women? And if that is so – why is it so? We adore them. I adore them. She is more than us. But is she Hamlet? Or is she a flower? Is a flower less than us? Is the sky more than us? Is it less? It makes you wonder, about all the women from the dawn of time. What we may have missed. Something, yes?

EDMOND. I have to do this for her! And I do not know how, I do not know how to take the poetry out of Hamlet and render him poetic nonetheless.

ALPHONSE. Isn't that her problem? Don't look at me like that; I'm not being merely provocative. Maybe there's already too much poetry in her. Maybe Shakespeare is competing with the Divine Sarah. Maybe she's right. Maybe Shakespeare is the one who needs to settle down.

EDMOND. I have not been put on this earth to settle down Shakespeare! I hate it. I mean it. I hate it. I feel like I'm covered in ink and I'm just putting my handprint everywhere and it's just ink everywhere and it's nothing. I end up with nothing.

ALPHONSE. *(Off the pages.)* You know you're not actually taking the poetry out. Just the, what do you call it – ba BA ba BA ba BA.

EDMOND. The iamb.

ALPHONSE. It's still poetry just without the ba BA ba BA ba BA.

EDMOND. That's not all that changes if you take the iamb out. How he makes the language soar is the might of who he is. It's prayer; it's incantation. It's enchantment. It's a hymn. It's grace itself. It's...

(A headshake, off his own work.)

This is more naturalistic, which is what she wants; it's what she wants. But it's not what Shakespeare did. It's not what he meant.

(Lights shift.)

Scene Three

*(**SARAH** is having a dinner party in her dressing room. She is dressed magnificently in a gorgeous gown. The critic **LOUIS** is there, being provocative. Also present: **ALPHONSE**, **EDMOND**, and **CONSTANT**. **SARAH** pours wine.)*

LOUIS. The celebrated American Mr. Mark Twain tells us "There are five kinds of actresses: bad actresses, fair actresses, good actresses, great actresses – and then there is Sarah Bernhardt."

CONSTANT. Certainly she would agree with him.

SARAH. *(Pleased.)* She would.

*(She kisses **CONSTANT**.)*

LOUIS. But the British are less kind. Mr. Shaw calls her acting "childishly egotistical."

CONSTANT. Everyone has an opinion.

LOUIS. He feels that she does not make her audiences feel or think more deeply, but rather she merely makes them admire her.

ALPHONSE. And they do admire her.

SARAH. That is not all I do.

LOUIS. I'm not finished.

SARAH. Mr. Shaw is always in a bad mood. He thinks he knows everything. He lives in his head, not his heart.

LOUIS. He thinks –

SARAH. That is all he does, is think. He sneers at the audience, at the fact that they want to feel things. He loves Duse, who just stands there, pretending she doesn't care about anyone's feelings but her own.

CONSTANT. He loved you in Camille.

CONSTANT, ALPHONSE & EDMOND. *(They cheer.)* Camille! Brava!

SARAH. Of course he loved me in Camille! All the men love the beautiful whore who is there to adore the prince and remind him of feeling and passion, then renounce him and conveniently die so he doesn't have to sully himself with tawdry melodrama anymore, when he needs to marry and pass on all that money to children who are, you know. Unsullied.

ALPHONSE. That – is a remarkably accurate assessment.

SARAH. Thank you, Alphonse.

LOUIS. What do you think Mr. Shaw will say when he hears she is taking on Hamlet?

SARAH. I don't care what he thinks. He's a snob. He's an egghead.

EDMOND. You need the eggheads to love you.

SARAH. They will love me! In your Hamlet, they will see me as they have never seen me before.

LOUIS. Oh, so it's Rostand's Hamlet now!

EDMOND. I do not say so.

> (**LOUIS** *decides to poke at it.*)

LOUIS. Hamlet has been rewritten before. All Shakespeare has fallen victim to the pen of a lesser writer at one time or another.

SARAH. I take exception to that.

LOUIS. I did not mean to offend.

EDMOND. No offense is taken. It is an honor to contribute in any way I can to Sarah's mighty endeavor.

LOUIS. Well, I think it's perverse.

> (*The others protest, but he is performing for them all now.*)

Hear me out; hear me out. All I'm saying is that our hostess is the most sensual woman the world has ever seen.

SARAH. Thank you, my friend.

> (*She curtsies to him.*)

LOUIS. And she means to play Hamlet, the least sensual man the world has ever seen.

SARAH. You say he is not sensual because he is never played that way. And it is nonsense. A youth of nineteen –

LOUIS. He is thirty.

SARAH. He is not thirty; why do men so desperately need him to be thirty?

LOUIS. I don't "need" him to be anything; it is what he is. When he picks up Yorick's skull –

SARAH. I cannot have this argument all over again. He is nineteen and he is ludicrous in the extremities of his circumspection. In the way only a self-obsessed youth can be, but he is a hero, a tragic hero we can all agree on that at least.

LOUIS. Well –

SARAH. Stop it, you know he is otherwise what are we doing here.

CONSTANT. What ARE we doing here?

SARAH. We are eating and drinking and arguing about the theater. He is young. He is vigorous.

LOUIS. He is tormented.

SARAH. Yes but how are we to feel his torment if the exquisite composition of his language stands in front of it?

LOUIS. Ah, this goes to the question of Rostand's contribution.

SARAH. It does. I have performed in Master Shakespeare's plays how many times.

LOUIS. Your Ophelia was divine. And your Cordelia.

SARAH. Thank you. No one has more reverence than I for the might of the mighty Shakespeare.

LOUIS. But.

SARAH. His gift for poetry at times overwhelms the power of his playwriting. The play wants translation.

LOUIS. "Translation" is a large word, but you give it a small meaning.

SARAH. How so?

LOUIS. Taking out the poetry?

SARAH. There are many kinds of poetry, and "translation" never has a small meaning. What is theater itself but a constant act of translation? We take a script; we imbue it with life. We translate everything in the theater, we invent what we will and translate the rest. Shakespeare was constantly translating other sources. All those history plays.

CONSTANT. Hollingshead.

SARAH. Yes.

CONSTANT. Plutarch.

SARAH. Plutarch!

CONSTANT. Heroditus.

SARAH. To hear some people tell it, Shakespeare never had an original thought in his head.

EDMOND. No one would say that.

SARAH. I just did. And it speaks to my point: Theater itself is an act of transformation. This is his subject. Transformation.

CONSTANT. And cross-dressing, my god he was obsessed with it. What? Isn't that what you're really bothered by? A woman playing a man?

LOUIS. It is a question.

CONSTANT. Not really. He loved it.

LOUIS. In the other direction.

SARAH. Is there a direction? Is there not just movement?

LOUIS. Women were not allowed on the stage –

EDMOND. What are we arguing about now?

SARAH. I don't know. It feels good though, I'm winning.

CONSTANT. Well, so the purists cry, "If the only object of the theater is amusement then make it an exhibition of women." I do not say so.

Not that I am opposed to exhibiting women, if art is to find a profit in it: that is to say if, by exhibiting them, we excite a purely theatrical pleasure in the spectator's breast, and not a pleasure of a lower, I might say, more shameful kind. Not that there is anything wrong with that either.

LOUIS. Here here. I was making a point. The act of looking at a woman is in its essence different than the act of looking at a man, is it not?

SARAH. Is it?

LOUIS. You know it is; you have made a fortune out of the fact that –

SARAH. *(Overlapping, to the others.)* I wish I had made a fortune.

LOUIS. *(Overlapping.)* – People cannot take their eyes off you once you're framed by that proscenium. But when you are outside of that proscenium who are you?

SARAH. I am myself.

LOUIS. You are a freak.

EDMOND. I beg your pardon?

(There is a silence at this.)

SARAH. It's all right.

EDMOND. It is not all right.

SARAH. Continue, please.

LOUIS. A woman with power is a freak. A freak of nature, perhaps, but a freak nonetheless. Shakespeare himself acknowledged it. "Unsex me here" is one of his mightiest condemnations. A woman reaching for power? It's unholy.

CONSTANT. That's a different play.

LOUIS. Titania is humiliated, bedded by an ass, for exerting her power.

CONSTANT. I've played Bottom. He's harmless, really. Very likeable.

LOUIS. Lear's daughters –

SARAH. *(Getting testy.)* Lear's daughters all come to foul ends, the good and the bad. As does Lear himself. Your point has muddled itself with overreach. I haven't heard a thing which truly argues against my playing the Danish prince. I think Shakespeare would understand it.

LOUIS. He would not understand rewriting his play.

SARAH. Well then let's not ask him, shall we? Trust me, my public will not be sorry that I choose to bring the great Hamlet to life without putting them through how many –

CONSTANT. Four, at least.

SARAH. Four hours of poetry. At least.

EDMOND. *(A caution.)* Shakespeare elevates with his poetry.

(**SARAH** *turns at that, startled.)*

LOUIS. Precisely, who are we to toss his creations back into the dirt.

SARAH. What's wrong with getting a little dirty?

LOUIS. *(To* **ALPHONSE***.)* And you, one assumes, are doing the poster?

ALPHONSE. I am.

LOUIS. Well, I suppose it's better than those little biscuit tins you design. How is it coming?

(*A beat. It's rather awkward. Luckily interrupted by a commotion offstage.)*

MAURICE. *(Offstage.)* No she does not know I'm coming, but I am here nonetheless! I think she will want to see me!

(He enters.)

SARAH. *(Startled.)* Maurice? Maurice –

MAURICE. Mother.

SARAH. When did you arrive?

MAURICE. Just now, from the train.
(To the others, short.) Hello. Coquelin, Alphonse, honored to see you.
(A little chillier.) Rostand.

SARAH. *(Warm, delighted.)* Come, come – join us! Do we have a plate for my son? You look thin. Have you been eating? Get him a plate!

MAURICE. Mother, what is this nonsense about Hamlet?

(A beat.)

CONSTANT. I don't know why everyone thinks it's such a bad idea. She's really very good.

MAURICE. It will ruin her!

SARAH. If I'm going to have to go through this again, I'm going to need another glass of wine.

MAURICE. Rumor has it that he is rewriting it for you!

SARAH. It is no rumor; it is fact.

MAURICE. Is that all he is doing for you?

SARAH. Have you met my friend, Monsieur Lamercier, the esteemed critic? He is thinking of writing about my Hamlet.

MAURICE. Honor to meet you.

(**LOUIS** *responds.*)

SARAH. My personal life is not a matter of public debate.

MAURICE. If that were true it would be the first time.

SARAH. Well, I will not be interrogated by my own son as if I were some kind of thief in the docket.

MAURICE. This is not a play, Mother!

SARAH. Clearly not since your acting is abysmal. I am ashamed to call you my child.

MAURICE. This is a disaster!

SARAH. I have lived through actual disaster, Maurice, as you well know. This is not that. And I am not arguing about this anymore.

MAURICE. Mother –

SARAH. Enough enough, enough ENOUGH.

(*This silences him, and the room.*)

Leave me please. All of you.

(*They all stand to go.*)

(*To* **MAURICE**.) Not you! The rest of you, go go go – Constant here one for the road.

(*She gives* **CONSTANT** *a bottle of wine as they all exit.* **EDMOND** *stops to talk to her. She shakes him off.*)

Come to me tomorrow.

(*He goes.* **MAURICE** *and* **SARAH**, *alone.*)

SARAH. And so the righteous son returns from university to berate his unworthy mother. Where have I heard that one before?

MAURICE. Have you no shame?

SARAH. No I don't! My lack of shame is legendary! People love that about me!

MAURICE. They will not love this.

SARAH. They will. My Hamlet will be as legendary as I am.

MAURICE. I'm not talking about Hamlet.

SARAH. Of course you are. It is all anyone is doing in Paris, talking about Hamlet. Which is fine because it is all Hamlet does, is talk about Hamlet.

MAURICE. What is going on with you and Rostand?

SARAH. *(Defiant.)* He is a great poet of the theater. He is our finest playwright. I have asked him to write a version of Hamlet for me, to give him more immediacy and less self-obsessed introspection. To make him more what he yearns to be: A man of action.

MAURICE. Aside from that being one of the worst ideas I've ever heard, that's not the whole story and you know it. Everyone is gossiping.

SARAH. Gossip is a good thing, it means that they're as usual fascinated by my charisma.

MAURICE. If he leaves his wife for you, it will be the one thing your charisma cannot conquer.

SARAH. You think the public would turn on me? You underestimate them. Have you forgotten I have had sexual relations with all the crowned heads of Europe. It's true; I seduced every one of them. Also, I am told, on "incontestable authority" that in addition to you, Maurice, I've given birth to four illegitimate sons, one by the Emperor of France, one by the Tsar of Russia and one by a man condemned to the guillotine for murdering his father, one by a hairdresser. I don't know where they are, wouldn't you like to meet them? I would! I feed quails to my pet lion. I force my seamstress to build my wardrobe on an army of skeletons. I eat mussels for lunch every day. If he left his wife for me they would be positively bored by it.

MAURICE. They would not be bored.

SARAH. No they wouldn't because I never bore. It is something that you can count on me for.

MAURICE. I love you, Mother.

SARAH. This is a peculiar way to show it. Barging in on my dinner party, embarrassing me before my guests –

MAURICE. *(Not apologetic.)* I apologize, I was hasty.

SARAH. Making my point for me, about the recklessness of youth. I'm glad you're here, I want to study a few things. There is such lightness and power in a young man's movement. Can you walk to me, so I can watch it a few times?

MAURICE. I'm not going to model Hamlet for you.

SARAH. Then what are you doing here?

MAURICE. You have been reckless before but nothing like this.

SARAH. Oh reckless.

MAURICE. Do you deny it? A year ago you were worth two million francs. Today, you have nothing.

SARAH. I don't have nothing, who told you I have nothing.

MAURICE. You did, in your last letter –

> *(He gets it out.)*

SARAH. That was weeks ago.

MAURICE. You sent this to me yesterday; it's why I came.

SARAH. *(Looking at it.)* I did send this, I was in despair. *(An admission.)* Oh, Maurice.

MAURICE. You cannot, you just cannot keep doing this, Mother.

SARAH. Keep doing what? Living?

MAURICE. You act like you have endless resources.

SARAH. I know.

MAURICE. You run through your money.

SARAH. When I have it, it seems like there is so much of it! And then –

MAURICE. And then you spend it.

SARAH. What else are you supposed to do with money. And there are so many interesting things to spend it on. Beautiful things.

MAURICE. But then you don't have it.

SARAH. But then there's always more out there.

MAURICE. You must –

SARAH. *(Stopping him.)* Don't – please, please don't say "must," it is an ugly word

MAURICE. You are not young anymore!

SARAH. I'm – oh – what? According to every person in this room tonight I am ageless.

MAURICE. And who paid for the dinner?

SARAH. What are you talking about, I paid for the dinner of course –

MAURICE. They are scavengers and hangers-on.

SARAH. *(A rebuke.)* They are my friends. I live for them.

MAURICE. You live for your audience! You live for your art! You live for the world!

SARAH. You say that as if it's a problem.

MAURICE. You need to live for yourself. And me.

(A beat.)

SARAH. You need money.

MAURICE. I did not come here to ask for money.

SARAH. And yet.

MAURICE. And yet if you weren't throwing it around so much, there would be a little more for me. And you.

SARAH. I have what I need.

MAURICE. Mother. You act like a queen. But you are not a queen! You are an actress.

SARAH. Just as good. Better. Sometimes you are the queen, throwing money around, and other times you're someone else altogether. As you say. You're not merely the queen, you're also an actress, and if you run out of money you can go on tour in America and make a bundle. And they pay for your meals there. They're very nice.

MAURICE. But you're not going on tour.

SARAH. *(Impatient.)* Because I don't want to go on tour, I want to play HAMLET.

MAURICE. You want everything.

SARAH. Which is not really a problem because I usually get it.

MAURICE. Nobody gets everything.

SARAH. Watch me.

MAURICE. And you know what? When women want everything? Men do not like it.

SARAH. Do I care what men like?

MAURICE. Do you not.

SARAH. You know you were more pleasant when you were a tiny boy, telling me you loved me all the time, that was frankly a little easier to take.

MAURICE. Mother, I am the one person who can say it because it is my truth and all in all I don't mind it. If you are everything, then what are we?

SARAH. You are everything – to me.

MAURICE. *(A smile.)* I know.

> *(She kisses him.)*

SARAH. *(Collapsing a little, finally.)* Oh, Maurice.

> *(He holds onto her, considers her. Finally all performance is gone and they are just a mother and son who love each other unconditionally.)*

MAURICE. How bad is the money situation?

SARAH. *(An admission.)* I don't know.

MAURICE. You don't know?

SARAH. Please don't yell at me.

MAURICE. I'm not yelling. But the theater is surely expensive.

SARAH. There are more seats. More tickets. More revenue.

MAURICE. If they come.

SARAH. They'll come.

MAURICE. They did not come to the last one.

SARAH. But in a larger house, Maurice. The lights are so much more forgiving. I understand it's a gamble.

MAURICE. Hamlet is more than a gamble.

SARAH. Hamlet is life.

MAURICE. What does that mean?

SARAH. It means what it means. Hamlet is unexpected. It is complicated. Unknowable.
Impossible.

MAURICE. Which is why you want to do it.

SARAH. Of course it is! How do people live without trying things that are impossible?

MAURICE. Somehow they do.

SARAH. If that's true, that is just, bizarre to me.

MAURICE. You know it's true and you also know it's not why I'm here. What's the story with Rostand?

SARAH. That's different.

MAURICE. It's not merely the charm of the impossible.

SARAH. No.

MAURICE. Oh, Mother.

SARAH. Oh, what?

MAURICE. He's so young. And a wife and two babies – not one but two little *babies* –

SARAH. Don't yell at me.

MAURICE. I am going to yell at you! You cannot love him.

SARAH. *(An honest admission.)* Oh, Maurice. I love him quite.

MAURICE. It was easier when you were infatuated with that actress, what was her name?

SARAH. Francine, she was a sculptress.

MAURICE. Francine.

*(They both mutually swoon over the memory
of Francine for a moment.)*

SARAH. This is no infatuation. He is half of me. More than
half. And I more than half of him. The self recognizing
the self. Shakespeare would know how to explain it, the
old bastard.

MAURICE. Oh, Mother.

SARAH. Be happy for me. Don't worry so much. Or if you
are going to worry, worry about money. Come back and
take care of it for me.

MAURICE. We tried that. I was terrible at it.

SARAH. You weren't!

MAURICE. The only person worse with money than you,
is me. You just gave me that job so that I would stick
around.

SARAH. It worked!

MAURICE. Until I lost all our money. I adore you, Mother. I
adore you.

SARAH. And I you, Maurice.

MAURICE. I beg you. Just think for once.

(A knock at the door.)

SARAH. Let me tell you something. Hamlet does nothing
but think. And it gets him nowhere.

*(The door opens and a woman appears,
looking around.)*

Can I help you?

ROSAMOND. Madame Sarah Bernhardt?

SARAH. Yes of course.

ROSAMOND. We have never met.

SARAH. I do not believe so madame and yet I find you here
in my dressing room, I cannot help but wonder why.

ROSAMOND. I am Rosamond Gérard. You know my
husband, I think. Edmond Rostand. Is he here?

SARAH. No, he's not. This is my son, Maurice.

MAURICE. Madame.

(He offers her a chair.)

ROSAMOND. No, thank you, I cannot stay.

MAURICE. Nor can I sadly. Goodnight Mother.

SARAH. Maurice I would love for you to stay.

MAURICE. Sadly, I cannot. Goodnight.

(He goes. The two women are alone.)

SARAH. This night.

(Then.)

I am sorry, I don't know what to say to you. Rostand was here for dinner with some others. We spoke of the work he is doing for me on Hamlet; perhaps you know of this. I cannot say because now he is gone. I presumed to his home to you and your children, perhaps he stopped on the way. I don't know.

ROSAMOND. You mistake me, madame. I am not here in search of my husband.

SARAH. No?

ROSAMOND. It is you I seek.

SARAH. Wonderful. Wonderful. Unfortunately, it is such a late hour.

ROSAMOND. I have a great favor to ask of you. And I did not know how else to do it.

SARAH. (Dry.) No?

ROSAMOND. My husband is enraptured by you.

SARAH. I am merely the instrument upon which his words are played.

ROSAMOND. You are Sarah Bernhardt. You are not a "mere" anything.

SARAH. There is some truth to what you say. Nonetheless

ROSAMOND. My husband is a great writer. I am a writer myself.

SARAH. Are you?

ROSAMOND. Poetry, mostly. Although I have written a play or two.

SARAH. Haven't we all.

ROSAMOND. "For you see, each day I love you more. Today more than yesterday and less than tomorrow."

SARAH. Well, thank you.

ROSAMOND. It's a couplet I wrote. In a poem. I wrote it for Edmond, of course.

SARAH. Of course.

ROSAMOND. It has achieved some small notoriety. They've made little medals out of it. People give them to their lovers as a sign of affection.

SARAH. How charming.

ROSAMOND. Sometimes I think, that tiny couplet is all I will ever be known for. If I'm known for anything. Aside from having married Edmond Rostand.

SARAH. You are too modest. "Each day I love you more. Today more than yesterday and less than tomorrow." Yes, it has a beautiful lilt to it. I'm sure you will have many more wonderful successes as a poet.

ROSAMOND. I'm content to be Edmond's wife, actually. I see who he is and what he can be. And I see how painful it is, what you do. The theater. He suffers so.

SARAH. Yes, suffering, of course. Is part of it. I suffer, we all suffer.

ROSAMOND. I think what a writer suffers is so deep and disorienting. The not knowing, where it will all come from. Starting with nothing and then creating whole worlds, out of nothing. Of course it's frightening. And he is so talented, Edmond. He is our greatest poet of the theater, now. I know you agree with me.

SARAH. I do; I do.

ROSAMOND. People say he is in love with you.

SARAH. No.

ROSAMOND. It is spoken of, everywhere.

SARAH. We love each other as artists. We create together. Sometimes people confuse that.

ROSAMOND. You think me confused?

SARAH. It is impossible to understand what intense joy steals over the actor when he feels that a trembling audience is hanging on his lips and his looks, while he knows that behind the scenes is a person who has erased, corrected, rejected words, sentences, and lines; who has so much at stake, his future, his glory, his all. Oh! We feel this heart that beats behind us even in our hearts, we hear it in our ears, and when at length the audience crowns the play with its approval, we experience the infinite enjoyment of the martyr at the extremity of his suffering, or of the lover in the realization of his dream. This sensation is denied the author. But it is so fugitive that he has no need to envy us. In fact, his work, which we have launched, soars higher and higher into the infinity of time.

ROSAMOND. Thank you for explaining that.

SARAH. You're welcome. Now, sadly, it is rather late and I do have an early rehearsal.

ROSAMOND. *(Ignoring that.)* He has been working so diligently on this new Hamlet.

SARAH. *(A shade of irritation finally.)* It is not a new Hamlet.

ROSAMOND. What is it?

SARAH. It is an "interpreted" Hamlet.

ROSAMOND. Hamlet but not Hamlet.

SARAH. Every production of every play is itself and not itself.

ROSAMOND. Is it?

SARAH. Every actor is different and so every interpretation of that character is different. My Hamlet is not Coquelin's Hamlet. My Medea is not Duse's. Thank god. And then, every night of every production is different.

ROSAMOND. But Edmond's Hamlet is not his Hamlet. It is Shakespeare's Hamlet. It will always be Shakespeare's Hamlet.

SARAH. Edmond's Hamlet will be our Hamlet.

ROSAMOND. It will not be spoken of that way. It will only be your Hamlet. Edmond's contribution to your success will be eclipsed. By you.

SARAH. Edmond cannot be eclipsed.

ROSAMOND. Edmond should not be eclipsed. But he can be. There is a difference.

SARAH. I understand your reservations – no, I don't understand them; people have been rewriting Shakespeare's plays since he wrote them in the first place so in fact I don't know what all the FUSS is about me doing it.

ROSAMOND. You aren't doing it; Edmond is doing it.

SARAH. Because he's the writer! And as you've pointed out he's the best playwright in Paris right now so of course he is the one who should help me craft this and he's being paid; I am paying him.

ROSAMOND. You haven't paid him yet.

SARAH. *(Frustrated.)* Writers don't get paid until the audience shows up, I didn't make up the rules! Why are you here, madame? Excuse me for being blunt but as I said I have an early rehearsal tomorrow and can you just tell me, please, what you have to say to me? What is it you want to know?

     (They consider each other.)

ROSAMOND. Edmond has a play.

SARAH. All playwrights do.

ROSAMOND. It is magnificent.

SARAH. All of his work is.

ROSAMOND. *(A laugh.)* That is not true of Edmond's work any more than it is true of your own.

SARAH. I beg your pardon.

ROSAMOND. And it is about you.

     *(This gives **SARAH** pause.)*

It gives me no pleasure to admit it. He thinks of nothing but you. He writes of nothing but you. And it is beautiful, it is his masterpiece. It will outlive all of us. And he has stopped writing it.

SARAH. Writers are unpredictable. The mood strikes them, it flees. And then it returns.

ROSAMOND. That is not what is happening to him. He is distracted by the task you set him. He spends his nights and days now, trying to give you what you want. A bastardized version of Hamlet.

SARAH. "Bastardized." What is wrong with a little rewrite?

ROSAMOND. Hamlet is killing him.

SARAH. Hamlet is killing me.

ROSAMOND. You are unkillable.

> *(This is said a little too sharply. **SARAH** turns at it. **ROSAMOND** takes a script out of her bag. She puts it on the table.)*

Just look at it. He must finish it. You must release him.

SARAH. Edmond is his own man. He does exactly as he chooses.

ROSAMOND. Read it.

SARAH. I will not read it.

ROSAMOND. It is about you. He is writing it for you. Read it.

> *(She goes. **SARAH** – angry, disturbed – paces for a moment. She eyes the manuscript.)*
>
> *(Blackout.)*

Scene Four

(Lights shift. The stage the following day.
SARAH, *at the table, with the manuscript,*
thinking. **EDMOND** *enters, sees her.)*

EDMOND. Sarah. I've been walking all night. About what I said at your dinner party in front of everyone, I owe you an apology.

SARAH. We don't need to talk about that. Your wife came to see me last night.

(A beat.)

EDMOND. Rosamond was here?

SARAH. Yes, we had a lovely chat. About your play.

EDMOND. What play?

SARAH. The play you are writing. She says you are writing it for me. Or, you were writing it for me before I interrupted you.

(She holds it up, shows it to him.)

EDMOND. She brought you the play.

SARAH. Yes, she did.

EDMOND. And you read it.

*(**CONSTANT** arrives.)*

SARAH. Coquelin! You're early.

CONSTANT. You sent for me and said, "Come early."

SARAH. And so you're here. Good. Rostand has a new play.

EDMOND. It's not finished.

SARAH. Let's just read some of it, see how it sounds.

CONSTANT. What is the part?

SARAH. I shall be playing Roxanne.

CONSTANT. And she is...

SARAH. A woman, beautiful beyond distraction.

CONSTANT. Of course.

SARAH. All men are bewitched by her. But especially one. Her cousin is a great soldier, a great poet, a great wit. He adores her from afar but he cannot speak of his love.

CONSTANT. Why not?

SARAH. His nose.

CONSTANT. What about his nose?

SARAH. It is rather large.

CONSTANT. So?

EDMOND. It is his pride, actually.

SARAH. Precisely so. He's afraid you see and she's become infatuated with his friend, Christian, who is beautiful and an idiot. So he has to make up things for Christian to say.

CONSTANT. Why would he do that?

EDMOND. *(Frustrated.)* He is a character in a play and it is a first draft.

SARAH. Don't make excuses, let's just hear it. You can play Christian. The doltish lover.

> *(She goes to* **EDMOND***, takes his hand, and goes to the bench where she has left the script. She hands it to him.)*

Evening falls. Let's sit. Speak on. I listen.

> *(***EDMOND*** looks at her, looks at the script, thinks of bolting. He decides not to. She points to the script.)*

EDMOND. Oh. I love you.

SARAH. Yes, speak to me of love.

EDMOND. I...love you.

SARAH. That's it. The theme. Now vary it.

EDMOND. I love you so.

SARAH. Yes, I know that. And?

EDMOND. And I should be so glad – so glad if you would love me! Tell me you do!

SARAH. I hoped for cream; you give me gruel. Tell me. How does your love possess you?

EDMOND. Utterly.

SARAH. And?

EDMOND. Your throat! I'd like to kiss it!

> *(She stands, impatient, looks at* **EDMOND***, who points to the script.)*

SARAH. I know what to do. I'm doing it.

EDMOND. I am grown stupid.

SARAH. And that displeases me as much as if you had grown ugly.

EDMOND. I…

SARAH. Yes, you love me, that I know. Adieu.

> *(She pushes him aside, flipping through pages.)*

And then she's gone for a while and then – let's get to Constant, shall we – here. I have it by memory. Constant you will need the words.

> *(She hands him the pages, then continues up the stairs.)*

And then she goes up to her room, and disappears and you've both lost her forever.

> *(They look at her.)*

You've lost me forever! Continue the scene, please!

> *(She gestures, and the two men look at the script.)*

EDMOND. Oh! I shall die!

CONSTANT. Speak lower!

EDMOND. I shall die.

CONSTANT. The night is dark.

EDMOND. Well?

CONSTANT. All can be repaired. Although you merit not. Stand there, you wretch, fronting the balcony.

EDMOND. But –

CONSTANT. Do it!

(He shoves **EDMOND**. *Above,* **SARAH** *turns, re-entering the scene.)*

SARAH. Who's that?

EDMOND. Christian!

SARAH. Oh. You?

EDMOND. I would speak with you.

SARAH. No, you speak stupidly. You love me no more.

EDMOND. *(Prompted by* **CONSTANT**.*)* You say – Great Heaven! I love no more? When I – love more and more.

SARAH. A little better. Barely.

EDMOND. *(Again.)* And more and more yet! My love has grown apace, rocked by the anxious beating of this poor heart, which a wanton Cupid has claimed as his cradle!

SARAH. If you deem that Cupid be so cruel, should you not have stifled the child held there?

EDMOND. *(Again.)* I tried, I tried! But this newborn child is a young Hercules!

SARAH. But your words are halting tonight. Why?

CONSTANT. This grows too difficult.

(He shoves **EDMOND** *aside, steps out.)*

Night has come. They search to find you in the gathering dusk.

SARAH. My words find you easily enough.

CONSTANT. 'Tis true, yes, my heart is wide, open, yearning to draw them home. But mine must struggle and climb –

SARAH. I will come down.

CONSTANT. No!

SARAH. Let me see you!

CONSTANT. No. No – 'Tis too sweet – The rare occasion, when our hearts can speak, our selves unseen, unseeing!

SARAH. Why, unseen?

CONSTANT. Because – half-hidden – half-revealed – you see the dark folds of my shrouding cloak, and I, the shimmering whiteness of your dress. I but a shadow, you a star! Do you know what this moment might hold for me? If ever I were eloquent –

SARAH. You were eloquent.

CONSTANT. Yet never 'til tonight has my speech sprung straight from my soul.

SARAH. And why not?

CONSTANT. Your eyes have beams that turn men dizzy.

SARAH. What of it?

(Lost in his own words, **EDMOND** *watches, rapt.)*

CONSTANT. Pardon me. 'Tis so sweet, so novel. To be at last sincere. 'Til now, my frozen heart, fearing to be mocked –

SARAH. Mocked?

CONSTANT. But when such a moment does come, when feeling love exists in us, ennobling, why then what words –

SARAH. What words indeed.

CONSTANT. All, all. I shall take all words that ever were, or weren't, or could or couldn't be, and in mad armfuls, not bouquets, I'll smother you in them. I love you! Your name is a golden bell hung in my heart and when I think of you I tremble and the bell swings and rings along my veins – Roxanne, Roxanne along my veins... Do you begin to understand? So late, do you understand me? Too fair the night, too fair the moment. That I should speak thus to you, and you should listen. Nothing is left to me now but to die. Have words of mine the power to make you tremble? Then let death come. 'Tis I, I myself, who has conquered thee.

(A pause.)

EDMOND. That's you, Sarah.

SARAH. Yes I realize I have a few more words and then there are pages and pages of Cyrano proclaiming his love at length. Very beautiful writing.

CONSTANT. I love it.

SARAH. Good. Then one of us does.

EDMOND. It is but an early draft.

SARAH. Good then you're still open to criticism. Your Roxanne is an idiot.

EDMOND. She is not an idiot.

SARAH. She cannot see the truth which is right before her eyes, she falls in love with this Christian, she is supposedly such a paragon then why cannot she see that he is a beautiful idiot? She is just like a man. Blinded by a pretty fool with no soul.

EDMOND. She is unfinished.

SARAH. That's good because as of now there is nothing to her at all.

EDMOND. Not yet, no. At this point in the story she is not the person she will become.

SARAH. She can't tell the difference between who is talking to her? She thinks this fool Christian suddenly has developed an astonishing gift for poetry?

EDMOND. Cyrano has been writing to her as Christian –

SARAH. Why.

EDMOND. You know why, because he is ashamed of his nose!

SARAH. His nose, what an idiot.

EDMOND. You cannot keep calling them idiots, Sarah.

SARAH. I can and I do. Both of them idiots. His nose is his impediment? His nose? He is afraid she will find him ugly, and not see his soul? Then why does he want her?

EDMOND. She comes to Christian, on the battlefield, and he –

SARAH. Oh yes I read that part. She comes to Christian, because his letters have made her love him even more, only the letters again are Cyrano –

EDMOND. Why are you so angry?

SARAH. I'm not angry. It's beautiful. She has no soul until he gives her one.

EDMOND. No, that is not –

SARAH. Your wife is more clever than you give her credit for.

EDMOND. I never said she wasn't clever.

SARAH. She brings your masterpiece to me, in the middle of the night, begging me to let you finish your play. It's for me, your new masterpiece is for ME she tells me.

EDMOND. It is for you!

SARAH. It is for Coquelin! Coquelin will be brilliant as your Cyrano. He will be brilliant. As I stand on the balcony. Adored.

(*A beat.*)

CONSTANT. I'm going to go smoke a cigarette.

SARAH. Please do.

(**CONSTANT** *goes.*)

EDMOND. I am sorry for offending you.

(*He's not.*)

SARAH. You would have me play her. Her.

EDMOND. What playwright does not dream of Sarah Bernhardt acting his words?

SARAH. Then you might consider giving me more of them.

EDMOND. You keep telling me to take them away in Hamlet!

SARAH. This is how you see me. As some divine – moron –

EDMOND. Roxanne is the embodiment of female perfection.

SARAH. If you like them pretty and silent.

EDMOND. If I liked them silent I would not be transfixed by you.

SARAH. (*Ignoring that, building steam.*) No wonder she doesn't love him. Your Cyrano is an egomaniac. He can't shut up.

EDMOND. My god. It is a first draft!

SARAH. And he is not prideful, as you suggest. He is a coward.

EDMOND. He is no coward.

SARAH. He does not act, he does not open his heart –

EDMOND. He has the biggest heart imaginable, what he does for her, for his men –

SARAH. Christian, who you present as a complete dolt, at least knows how to take a woman into his arms!

    (There is a pause at this.)

Well?

EDMOND. *(Searching for a pen.)* It's a good line. May I take a moment to write it down?

SARAH. No you may not! You may not use me to inspire you.

EDMOND. I'm not allowed to be inspired by you now?

SARAH. Not if all you can do is use me up as some statue for you to throw your genius poetry at.

EDMOND. If anyone is being used up in this agreement –

SARAH. Agreement! I agree to nothing.

EDMOND. – It is me. You tell me that I am the greatest playwright of our time and then you want me to take whatever gifts I have and and and annihilate them in service to your – demented idea –

SARAH. *(Enraged.)* Demented?

EDMOND. That to make you a decent Hamlet we must destroy him. And destroy me in the doing.

SARAH. That is a disgusting thing to say.

EDMOND. It is a disgusting thing to do. You have consigned me to the worst prison of any imagination, I could be bounded in a nutshell and count myself king of infinite space were it not that I have bad dreams about what a terrible writer I am next to Shakespeare. It is hell living in his mighty head.

It is hell thinking that my greatest achievement next to Hamlet is nothing. And you put me there. Every day. Every day, I stare at the most beautiful writing the world has seen. Is likely to see. Ever. And you ask me to destroy it. For you! For my love of you. And for your ego! For your fear! And I cannot use my gift for any of it. I cannot do it.

SARAH. *(Calm.)* My ego. My fear. My beauty. My light. My divinity. You dissect me with your words.

EDMOND. I love you with my words.

SARAH. And yet you cannot see yourself in a woman, I am not of you, I cannot be OF you –

EDMOND. Oh what are we arguing about now?

SARAH. "I cannot separate what you are and what I am, one from the other anymore." These are your words. You said them to me. We are the same. You said this. I am your voice.

EDMOND. I did say that, Sarah.

(She gestures to the pages, uncomprehending.)

SARAH. Then how can you write this? How can you put all your genius into Cyrano and make Roxanne this empty vessel?

EDMOND. *(Angry and hurt by that.)* That is what you think.

SARAH. This is what I know.

EDMOND. And this is what I know: You want to be a man.

SARAH. I do not want to be a man.

EDMOND. You crave a man's power.

SARAH. No man has more power than I do.

EDMOND. Shakespeare does.

SARAH. Shakespeare has more than power. He has strength. And I match him for that. And I will not go back to playing flowers for you fools. Not because I am too OLD. But because I was never a flower, and no matter how much you loved how beautifully I might play the ingénue, it was always beneath me. It is beneath all women.

EDMOND. Then rise to the challenge you have set yourself and play Hamlet! As he is written. Submit!

SARAH. Submit?

EDMOND. Submit to Shakespeare.

SARAH. That word "submit" always seems to show up in the most unfortunate moments. I know who I am, and what I am doing. I am completely capable of saying all the words as written and playing him as written. I know how Macready did it and how Irving did it and how Coquelin did it. I am creating a new Hamlet. There will be other Hamlets. But I will not be told that I cannot create my Hamlet. A Hamlet who is vital and fierce. He kills them all! My Hamlet will act!

EDMOND. Hamlet's tragedy is that he can*not* act. He speaks, gloriously. Cyrano in his wildest dreams cannot speak as Hamlet does. That is my tragedy.

>*(It pains him to say it. As long as he's out there on the limb, he decides to go all the way.)*

And now we come to your tragedy.

SARAH. I am not a tragic figure.

EDMOND. You are Sarah Bernhardt. But Sarah Bernhardt is a woman. And people do not want to see a woman play Hamlet.

SARAH. I do not play him as a woman! I play him as MYSELF.

>*(Then.)*

Where is his greatness? Where? Is it not in his mind, his soul, his essence? Where is mine? What is it about me you love? Because if in our essence we are the same, why am I otherwise less?

EDMOND. I did not say that.

SARAH. Did you not?

>*(Then.)*

Your play is good. It is beautiful. But Roxanne should not be silenced in order for your Cyrano to speak. You think you are worshipping her, but you're actually worshipping yourself.

EDMOND. That is a terrible distortion.

SARAH. In which case we have both disappointed each other utterly today.

>*(It is a stalemate. **SARAH** finally goes, gets the script, and hands it to him.)*

EDMOND. Sarah.

SARAH. Your wife is a genius. She has outwitted us both.

> (*Heartbroken, she goes.* **EDMOND** *looks at the pages he is left with as the stage shifts and Cyrano rises around him.*)

> (**CONSTANT** *enters, as Cyrano, with rapier. He turns on* **FRANÇOIS**. *His nose is huge. The play unfolds as* **EDMOND**, *in the center, watches and guides it.*)

CONSTANT. Go! Or rather tell me why you look so sharply at my nose.

FRANÇOIS. What! I...

CONSTANT. Is there anything extraordinary about it?

FRANÇOIS. Your lordship mistakes...

CONSTANT. Is it soft and swinging like an elephant's trunk?

FRANÇOIS. I did not say...

CONSTANT. Or crooked like the beak of an owl?

FRANÇOIS. No, I...

CONSTANT. Is there a wart on the end of it? Or a fly? What's amiss with it? Or is it a phenomenon?

FRANÇOIS. I didn't even look at it!

CONSTANT. Why shouldn't you look at it? Is it repulsive?

FRANÇOIS. My dear Sir...

CONSTANT. In color unhealthy? In shape indecent?

FRANÇOIS. Not at all!

> (*The other actors have gathered and are egging this on.*)

CONSTANT. Why, then, seem to revile it? Perhaps the gentleman finds it rather – large?

FRANÇOIS. I find it small, very small.

RAOUL. This gentleman is getting tiresome! He is a braggart!

> (*The crowd gasps.*)

> (*To the room.*) You...you have a nose – a nose, sir – that is indeed – very large.

(The room stops as Cyrano turns on him.)

CONSTANT. Very large, indeed! Is that all?

RAOUL. Well, I...

CONSTANT. No no that's a little too short young man – you might have said –

EDMOND. Well, many things!

CONSTANT. Yes many things in different keys. For instance, listen:

EDMOND. Aggressive:

CONSTANT. I sir had I such a nose, would at once have it amputated!

EDMOND. Friendly:

CONSTANT. It must dip into your glass. To drink with comfort, you should have a sling constructed.

EDMOND. Descriptive:

CONSTANT. It is a rock! A peak! A headland! More than a whole headland – a peninsula!

EDMOND. Inquisitive:

CONSTANT. What may this oblong thing be used for? A writing desk or a tool chest?

EDMOND. Pleasant:

CONSTANT. Do you love the little birds so much that you offer them so comfortable a resting place?

EDMOND. Pedantic:

CONSTANT. For so much flesh, on so much bone beneath the forehead we must go back, sir, to the animal Aristophanes calls Hippocampelephantocamelos!

EDMOND. Dramatic:

CONSTANT. When it bleeds –

EDMOND & CONSTANT. The Red Sea!

CONSTANT. That is about what you might have said, if you had a sprinkling of wit. Of wit, though you never had an atom and as to letters, you never had but the four that spell the word FOOL.

(He parries with his sword and the two men fence. The crowd cheers, then drifts away.)

*(***CONSTANT*** takes a bow. He gestures to **EDMOND**, who also bows to wild applause. As the applause rises around him, his expression shifts. The triumph has come at a cost.)*

(Blackout.)

Scene Five

(*The empty stage.* SARAH, *alone in light, as Hamlet.*)

SARAH. Thou woulds't not think how ill all's here about my heart: but it is no matter. It is but foolery; but it is such a kind of gain-giving, as would perhaps trouble a woman.

(*Shaking that off.*)

We defy augury; there's a special providence in the fall of a sparrow. If it be now, 'tis not to come; if it be not to come, it will be now; if it be not now. Yet it will come: the readiness is all.

(MAURICE *comes up behind her.*)

MAURICE. Mother?

(SARAH *turns, smiles at him.*)

SARAH. Maurice! What's the news?

(*She kisses him and goes to pick up two rapiers.*)

MAURICE. All of Paris is buzzing. Cyrano is a great success.

SARAH. As it should be. It is a wonderful play. A little too much obsession with the nose if you ask me; it always sounds so, well, you know what it sounds like. Men and their members.

(*Then.*)

Cyrano is a wonderful play. I'm sure Coquelin has never been better. And that's saying something as he is always very good.

MAURICE. Apparently they applauded for an hour.

SARAH. Astonishing.

(*He hugs her. She holds on to him, appreciating the comfort he offers.*)

MAURICE. I've read the new Hamlet. Eugene Morand and Marcel Schwob?

SARAH. It was too big a task for one person, as it turns out.

MAURICE. It's good.

SARAH. I think so too.

MAURICE. They say –

SARAH. Oh Maurice please don't tell me what they say. I am so bored by what they say.

MAURICE. All right.

(He picks up a rapier, tries it out.)

SARAH. All right, what do they say.

MAURICE. They say Rostand's next play is being written for you.

SARAH. *(Uninterested.)* Oh, really.

MAURICE. L'Aiglon. It is about the son of Bonaparte. Napoleon the second, the Eaglet they called him. Raised in captivity after his father was captured and the empire fell.

SARAH. And I'm meant to be his adoring and adorable nursemaid I suppose. Well, I will not do it.

MAURICE. You are meant to play the Eaglet. It is a breeches part. Written for you. A middle-aged woman playing the part of a boy. Audacious. They say it is a wonderful play.

SARAH. I will decide if it is wonderful.

MAURICE. Of course.

(ALPHONSE enters with poster.)

ALPHONSE. It's finished. God help me, I finished it finally. It's very good. Well, good, who am I to say. But I think it captures...something.

(He unfurls it for them. They all take it in.)

SARAH. I like it.

ALPHONSE. Do you?

SARAH. He eludes.

ALPHONSE. He does. But I think...

SARAH. *(Moved.)* Yes. He is looking for his father.

ALPHONSE. Yes. The ghost that haunts him, but doesn't take over the poster.

SARAH. Thank you, my friend.

> *(She turns to give it back to him.)*

ALPHONSE. No, keep it! I have to go back to the printer and oversee every copy. The ink keeps running to orange.

> *(He goes. **SARAH** turns to engage with **MAURICE**. They fence for a moment. She touches him.)*

MAURICE. A hit, a palpable hit!

SARAH. You are rusty.

> *(They begin to move back to first positions.)*

MAURICE. Does it bother you, ever?

SARAH. What?

MAURICE. A play lives through time. An actor's name is writ on water.

> *(She looks at him, thinks about that. He immediately regrets having asked it.)*

But you are Sarah Bernhardt. It is not true for you, of course.

SARAH. I am Sarah Bernhardt. Like all actors, I am air.

> *(She swings her sword.)*

But you know. There is a new kind of photograph. It moves.

MAURICE. It moves?

SARAH. It captures not words, but action. It captures life. Light.

> *(Then.)*

It will capture me.

> *(She is poised.)*

MAURICE. Nothing can capture you, Mother.

> *(She laughs at that and raises her rapier. The lights shift as she moves into the fight. Behind, the flickering strobe of the silent movie to come* reveals Sarah as Hamlet in his swordfight with Laertes as* **SARAH** *lunges with the sword, practicing the fight with her son.)*

> *(Fade to black.)*

End of Play

**Le Duel d'Hamlet*, 1900

CPSIA information can be obtained
at www.ICGtesting.com
Printed in the USA
LVHW081530221120
672388LV00013B/1943

9 780573 708091